"I'm sorry I made you uneasy yesterday. I let a personal matter affect my reaction to your generous offer, and I apologize."

Hannah waited for details, but Jude didn't offer them. "I'm sorry if I offended you." She still couldn't imagine how an offer of a free photo shoot would offend, but obviously it was possible.

"It was my fault alone." He hesitated, and Hannah searched his gaze, eager to see his secrets but not sure why it mattered so much. She quickly looked away. She had no business teasing herself with the attraction she felt. It was surely one-sided.

"Thanks for saying so." She drew a deep breath, forcing herself to meet his gaze. Then she realized she'd just provided him with a full view of her scarred cheek, and she looked the opposite way.

Jude's gaze followed the motion, and a flush rode up Hannah's neck. Definitely one-sided. He had no reason to be attracted to her, and a three-inch reason not to.

Books by Betsy St. Amant

Love Inspired

Return to Love
A Valentine's Wish
Rodeo Sweetheart
Fireman Dad
Her Family Wish

BETSY ST. AMANT

loves polka-dot shoes, chocolate and sharing the good news of God's grace through her novels. She has a bachelor's degree in Christian communications from Louisiana Baptist University and is actively pursuing a career in inspirational writing. Betsy resides in northern Louisiana with her husband and daughter and enjoys reading, kickboxing and spending quality time with her family.

Her Family Wish
Betsy St. Amant

Love Inspired

 ™ LOVE INSPIRED BOOKS

ISBN-13: 978-0-373-81616-3

HER FAMILY WISH

Copyright © 2012 by Betsy St. Amant

www.LoveInspiredBooks.com

Printed in U.S.A.

And we know that all things work together for good
to those who love God, to those who are the called
according to His purpose.
—*Romans* 8:28

To my grandmothers,
Marie Raney and Jo McLemore, not just for being
my biggest fans, but for building and leaving a
Christian legacy I can cling to. I am blessed.

Acknowledgments

Special thanks to Hannah Hough
of Hannah Hough Photography, who not only
took awesome author shots of me for my website,
but gave me insight into the world behind the
camera. Any errors in technical descriptions
are mine alone. Thanks for letting me
copy your first name, profession and haircut!
And to Sarah Rose, for her friendship and
brainstorming about hunky principals.
Also thanks to my agent, Tamela Hancock Murray
of The Steve Laube Agency, for being exactly what
I need during every phone call or email; and to
Emily Rodmell, editor extraordinaire, for your help
in nudging this book where it needed to go.

Chapter One

The only thing Hannah Hart hated more than mirrors was the spotlight.

"Class, this is Ms. Hart."

Hannah stared at the rows of young teenagers staring back at her, and offered a tentative smile as her best friend and art teacher, Sophia Davis, continued her glowing introduction.

"Ms. Hart is the owner of Hannah Hart Photography." She rambled on about Hannah's business and achievements. The kids didn't look all that impressed. One blew a bubble with her gum, which Sophia quickly confiscated with a piece of paper.

Hannah crossed her arms awkwardly over her navy suit jacket, feeling her face heat even as her skin grew clammy. Being a photographer didn't exactly qualify her to teach photography to a junior high fine arts class, but when Sophia had pleaded with Hannah to come, she couldn't say no. How could Hannah turn down the chance to share her lifelong love of photography with a whole set of potential future photographers?

Even if they were staring at her like she was some sort of sideshow.

Your scar isn't going anywhere, Hannah. You might as well get used to it. The car wreck that left a jagged line from her cheekbone to her chin might have happened two years ago, but the effects lingered. She pressed a hand to her stomach. All of the effects.

"Let's try to show her a little more respect than you guys show me, huh?" Sophia winked at the students as she tossed the gum-filled paper in the wastebasket, and a few of them giggled.

A petite blonde teen in the front row caught Hannah's eye, her hair plaited in thick braids. She wore a plaid dress that seemed severely old-fashioned compared to the stylish appearance of the other girls. Still, the outdated look didn't take away from her striking blue eyes and naturally thick lashes, all set within a cheekbone structure that would make many models jealous.

Hannah instinctively turned her head, tilting her good side toward the kids. Surely none of them would ask her about her scar. She was used to young children in their innocence and naïveté asking personal questions while on a photo shoot, but this was different. These kids were old enough to know better—she hoped.

"Hannah brought her camera today to show us

a little about the technical side of photography."
Perched on the edge of her desk, Sophia motioned
for Hannah to take center stage—as if it were that
easy. Maybe if Hannah's skin was as flawless as
her best friend's, her confidence level would be
a few notches higher. But that wasn't fair. She
wouldn't wish her insecurities on her worst enemy,
much less the friend who walked Hannah through
the first weeks after her accident.

Sophia pointed a finger at the kids. "Any questions you have along the way, go ahead and ask—
by raising your hand."

Hannah swallowed the nerves rising in her throat
and hoped her smile appeared more natural than
it felt. *They're just kids, Hannah. You photograph
them all the time.* The reminder did little to ease
her anxiety. Kids still had eyes—judging, questioning, curious eyes.

"Hey, guys." Her greeting came out froggier than
she intended. Hannah quickly cleared her throat,
then pulled her Nikon from her camera bag. Simply
holding the equipment in her hands gave her an
emotional boost, and she looped the strap around
her neck for safety before holding it out before the
class.

"This is a photographer's best friend—her
camera," Hannah said. She pointed to each part as
she defined the various terms. "And over here is
a self-timer." Not that she used that feature much

anymore. She preferred staying behind the camera to being on film herself these days.

"Can we hold it?" a brunette girl asked without raising her hand.

Hannah's mouth opened with uncertainty, but Sophia quickly intervened. "Not on your life. Next question?" She gestured to a boy in the second row. "Kent?"

"How much do photographers get paid?" He grinned, his freckles streaming together across his cheeks.

"That all depends on if a photographer works for a company or as an individual." Hannah smiled back, feeling a bit of tension finally ease from her neck with the honest questions—that didn't involve her face. "Of course we could chalk it up to not enough, and leave it at that."

The pretty blonde she'd noticed earlier actually raised her hand, the first one to do so, and Sophia pointed at her. "Go ahead, Abby."

Abby brought her arm back down to her side. "Are we going to discuss lighting soon? I don't have a real camera, just the one on my phone. But I always seem to get shadows in the wrong place when I take pictures with my friends."

Hannah nodded, impressed with the depth of her question. "We'll discuss lighting techniques before the end of the course. That's one of the most important aspects of photography."

"Good." Abby sat back in her chair, excitement shining in her eyes. "Thanks."

Such a polite kid. Looking at Abby and the rest of the class, Hannah felt like she was staring at a page from her favorite childhood magazine. *Which of these does not belong?* Not only in appearance, but in intellect, manners and decorum. Abby seemed like she'd be a ray of sunshine during this course compared to the other students, judging by the disinterested expressions on the majority of faces.

Hannah finished her presentation and when the bell rang, Sophia dismissed the class without giving any homework. "Don't think this is a habit," she hollered over the sound of notebooks being crammed into backpacks and the scraping of chairs on the worn floor.

A multitude of groans echoed in the students' wake, and Sophia turned to Hannah with a sheepish grin. "So some are more interested than others. What can I say?"

"They'll warm up." Hannah packed her equipment in her camera bag and rested the bag on Sophia's wooden desk. "Besides, didn't you say you only needed me once or twice a week?"

"Not that you're counting," Sophia teased. "But yes, that's what I said. We'll see if I meant it." She winked. "Don't forget you promised to help me carry over some of the lessons and applications into CREATE so we can get more hands-on—at least with the kids who want to."

CREATE was an after-school club Sophia had started last year that was a big hit with some of her more motivated students, the ones who wished to dive deeper into the fine arts. Hannah smiled. "I won't forget. Today might not be the best indicator of group interest, but some seemed more into it than others. Abby actually looked excited about it all."

"She's a good egg." Sophia slid several colored binders into a tie-dyed tote bag. "Most of the time, anyway."

Hannah frowned. "What do you mean? She was an angel today compared to the rest."

"Her father is Judah Bradley, the assistant principal. That doesn't exactly make her class favorite." Sophia shrugged, her curly red hair cascading around her shoulders. "Besides that, I think she's finally starting to realize she's *Little House on the Prairie* compared to the other girls, if you know what I mean."

"Well, she's beautiful regardless." Hannah rested her weight against the desk. That was the other thing that made Abby stand out from the rest of the girls in the class—she didn't seem to realize how gorgeous she was. From Hannah's side of the camera, that was almost unheard of. Most teens wanted to cake on the makeup and reveal as much as possible, not realizing the depth of their young beauty was still natural.

Sophia tugged the straps of her tote over her shoulder. "Jude's a single dad, and she's at that age now where they're butting heads over everything. I've overheard more than a few teachers discussing conversations *they've* overheard."

"It could be rumors," Hannah pointed out. She'd had enough of those to last a lifetime.

Sophia shrugged. "Either way, it's obvious they're having a rough time of it lately. But thankfully Abby's a really smart kid."

"I think so, too." A deep baritone sounded from the open door of the room, and Hannah jerked upright as a man in a dark suit strolled toward them. His sandy brown hair, short and gelled, brought out the deep blue of his eyes that had obviously been passed down to Abby. He shoved his hands casually in his pockets as he came to a stop beside Sophia. "Are you going to introduce me to your new assistant, or just discuss my family life?" A soft smile took the edge off his words, though his expression still meant business.

"Principal Bradley, I'm so sorry." A rare blush crept up Sophia's neck and Hannah felt one of her own crawling up her chest. "This is Hannah Hart."

"Nice to meet you." Jude extended his hand. "Please, call me Jude."

Hannah shook it, and an instant spark jolted from her wrist to her elbow. She quickly pulled her hand back and forced a smile, hoping the blush hadn't made its way to her ears yet. A red face only made her scar that much more obvious.

"Nice to meet you, too, Jude." His name rolled off her lips too easily, and her stomach churned a reaction she hadn't felt in years. *Don't be ridiculous, Hannah. You were caught gossiping about him. You don't stand a chance.* Not that any man that looked like Jude would glance at her twice anyway, unless they were ogling her scar. Her ex-fiancé had made that clear enough.

He crossed his arms over his dress shirt. "How was the first class on photography?"

"I think it went pretty well, considering." Hannah willed her stomach to settle. "Some of the kids seemed more interested than others." She gestured to Sophia. "We were discussing how attentive Abby was."

"Glad to hear it. She's a good student." Jude nodded briskly. "And it was nice of you to volunteer to do this for our school. I'm sorry we can't pay you for your help."

"I'm happy to do it," Hannah answered honestly. Maybe she wasn't so thrilled at first, but she couldn't help but feel especially happy about it now while standing in front of Jude. His gaze lingered on hers for a moment, and despite his polite smile and clean-shaven, professional appearance, a shadow lingered in his eyes. Hannah tilted her head to one side, recognizing the emotion she'd lived with for years—regret. She couldn't even imagine the struggles of life as a single parent, much less as a single dad. No wonder Abby seemed so out of fashion. Jude probably had his hands full keeping them above water, never mind trying to pay attention to the latest styles.

Eager to brighten Jude's obviously overworked day and make up for her embarrassing gossip blunder, Hannah gestured toward her camera bag. "I couldn't help but notice how photogenic your daughter is. I'd love to do a portrait session with her, for free of course—or even a family photo, if you'd be interested. It'd be great for my portfolio." Not to mention their own personal collection of memories. She doubted family pictures were something a single dad would think of keeping up with over the years. Her excitement grew at the idea of helping them out. "Would you be interested?"

Jude's smile slowly faded and his eyes darkened as a sudden storm clouded the depths of blue. "No, I wouldn't. But thanks."

Shock cemented Hannah's mouth shut, and before she could react, Jude turned and nodded at Sophia. "See you ladies tomorrow." Then he strode away as quickly as he'd appeared.

Chapter Two

Jude slid into the driver's seat of his silver sedan beside Abby, mentally kicking himself as he fastened his seat belt and fished for the key. Talk about a bad first impression. He'd practically snapped at Ms. Hart—Hannah—over nothing at all, at least as far as she was concerned. She couldn't have known that nothing was indeed something. He'd been hurrying past the art room on his way to his office when he'd heard Abby's name from inside. The entire incident was his own fault for eavesdropping, but he had a right to know what teachers—and volunteers—were saying about his daughter.

Especially lately, with Abby's first hint of teenage rebellion jump-starting like a Camaro off the line. A too-familiar headache pinched Jude's temples, and he rubbed his forehead before cranking the engine.

From the passenger seat, Abby quirked a curious eyebrow. He tried not to notice the Look with a capital *L* and forced what he hoped resembled a carefree smile. "Sorry I'm late. Forgot something in my office." And had been more than a little sidetracked along the way. He backed out of the parking lot, ready to get home and get out of his suit—and away from the memories of Hannah's beautiful smile. "How was your day?"

Abby zipped the backpack shut at her feet and wrangled into her seat belt, ignoring the question and jumping straight into the obvious. "What's wrong with you?"

He clenched his jaw. "Just a stressful day, honey." He couldn't tell Abby he'd snapped at a teacher's assistant—not exactly the role model image he kept desperately trying to project.

Residual anger at his ex boiled in his stomach. *Miranda, how could you put me in this position?* Not that she could hear him anymore from whichever gravesite in California she resided in. In fact, she hadn't heard a word he'd said ever since their jaunt down the aisle when they were practically teenagers themselves.

He drew a deep breath to clear his head. "More budget issues. The usual." It wasn't a lie. The strained school budget was stretching to the point of snapping like a rubber band, and he couldn't help but flinch every time he came near the paperwork—or Head Principal Coleman, who had sent an email today indicating one of the school electives would be cut.

"I saw you go into Ms. Davis's room after school." Abby twisted in her seat to face him as he pulled onto the frontage road. "Did you meet Ms. Hart?"

Jude kept his eyes on the traffic, partly for safety but mostly because he knew Abby's game. Her slightly-higher-pitched-than-usual tone proved she was feeling him out about the pretty new assistant. She'd used the same pitch about her fourth grade gym coach, her fifth grade room mother, and her sixth grade math teacher. Matchmaking ran thick in Abby's blood—yet made *him* want to run the other way. He'd dated here and there, but no one had been worth risking his heart over. It looked like his dream of having a big family would have to wait a little while longer. He might be over Miranda, but the effects of the woman lingered like a bad perfume.

"Yes, I met her." He kept his voice level, even as traitorous thoughts of Hannah flitted in his mind. His hands tightened on the wheel. So what if she was attractive? So what if her silky dark hair danced across her shoulders with each turn of her head? So what if her eyes shone such a rich brown it took him a full minute before he noticed the three-inch scar marring her cheek?

None of that mattered. Hannah took pictures for a living, and now taught the skill to the students—to his Abby. His stomach clenched as he flipped on his blinker. If this wasn't a credit-counting elective and if missing several weeks wouldn't set Abby back to the point of likely failing, he'd pull her out to avoid the whole photography unit. But that would raise questions—no one would understand why.

Especially not Abby.

"Did you think she was nice?" Abby pressed, yanking the tie off one of her braids and combing her hair with her fingers.

"I only spoke with her for a minute, sweetie." Long enough to know he was glad this was a temporary course. He could grit his teeth for a few weeks and make the best of it. Surely Abby wouldn't be corrupted to the point of becoming like her mother in less than a month—right? After all, photography wasn't modeling. But it was close enough to make him uneasy. What if Abby learned so much about the behind the scenes part that she decided she wanted to learn about being in *front* of the camera, too?

That would be the first step of many—and one he couldn't allow.

Abby flipped the visor down to check her reflection in her mirror. She rubbed her bare face with her fingers and sighed. "Lindsey was wearing makeup today."

Jude fought the automatic parental response threatening to roll off his tongue about friends and bridge jumping. "We've talked about this before, Abby. Twice, actually."

"But it doesn't make sense." Abby shut the visor with a snap as Jude pulled into the driveway of their modest, ranch-style home. "Most of the girls in my class wear makeup now. I'm almost thirteen."

"You don't need makeup." Jude hoped his voice conveyed the same finality he felt in his heart. "And you won't be thirteen for a few months." Three and a half, to be exact, and he was clinging to every last second. Although it felt like Abby had been a teenager for at least a year already. He shifted into Park and turned off the ignition. And to think he used to dread the terrible twos.

Abby made no move to get out of the car. "I'm not talking about black eyeliner and hot pink lipstick. Just a little lip gloss and mascara."

Maybe that was all for now. But as Miranda taught him, inches gave way to miles, and if Jude gave in today, Abby would be on the fast track to false eyelashes and stilettos. Begging to wear makeup would lead to begging for professional head shots and the next thing he knew, he'd have created a monster.

Again.

"Don't push this. My decision stands." Jude tugged off his seat belt, exhaustion knotting his neck.

She snorted. "If my mother were still alive she'd—"

"Abby!"

"What? It's not my fault she died when I was little. You never want to talk about her, and that's almost as annoying as your stupid rules."

Abby might have the details wrong, but the main truth of that statement smacked Jude in the stomach like a boxing glove. She was right—he *didn't* want to talk about Miranda. Didn't want Abby to know the truth about her mom. The mother figure she'd made up in her head all these years had kept Abby from feeling rejected, kept her from insecurities she shouldn't have to face at such a young age.

It just made Jude the bad guy.

Her tirade finished, and knowing she'd crossed a line, Abby wisely remained silent as she unbuckled her seat belt and threw open the car door. She stomped up the stone walkway to the house, where she waited with her back rigid for him to come with the keys.

Jude took his time pulling his briefcase from the backseat, giving them both a little space to cool off. Maybe he was being strict, but Abby didn't understand. If she knew what her mother had done, had become, she'd get it. But he couldn't tell her now, not during this sensitive time in her life. The teen years were hard enough without discovering your mother abandoned you as a kid because she preferred the bright lights and airbrushed pages of modeling to motherhood—and the recreational drugs that flowed in abundance and were her ultimate demise.

No, Abby shouldn't have to deal with the same pain Jude spent nearly a decade muddling through. Since she didn't have any memories of Miranda, Jude had mercifully put off the questions over the years, being just vague enough for Abby to draw her own conclusions. It was close enough.

And much better than the truth.

Hannah felt funny peering in the door to the teachers' lounge, as if she were once again a student wondering what on earth the adults did in there all day. She wasn't a kid anymore, but she wasn't an official staff member, either, so the unease lingered.

She poked her head around the frame of the mostly deserted room and looked for Sophia, who said to meet her during her break before the last period. Hopefully Jude wouldn't be inside. She couldn't bear to face him yet after the awkward conversation from Monday. Hannah's eyes darted anxiously to each table. Did assistant principals even use the lounge? Sophia waved from a corner table, and Hannah exhaled in relief as she made her way over.

"Decaf coffee? Stale donut?" Sophia pointed with a laugh to the unappealing array of leftovers, sitting on the counter by the sink cluttered with mugs.

Hannah made her way toward her, ducking her head to hide her scarred cheek as she passed a table of teachers hunched over what seemed to be lesson plans. "As, uh, tempting as that is, no thanks." She smiled and adjusted the strap on her camera bag. "How has the rest of the week gone?"

"They're slowly getting into it." Sophia brushed some crumbs off the table, then crumpled her napkin and tossed it into the trash can. "They stopped asking ridiculous questions, at least."

Hannah grinned. "That's a start." She tapped her bag. "I brought a lot of sample photos on lighting like you asked—even some pretty bad ones I saved from my practice days to show them the difference."

"See, this is why I need you! You're so much better than a textbook." Sophia grabbed her purse and motioned for Hannah to follow her out the door. "Let's go set up. The bell will ring in about ten minutes."

They quickly laid out Hannah's various photos and handouts, finishing as the bell rang. Students laughed and pushed their way inside the classroom, excited to get the last class of their Friday over with now that weekend freedom danced just out of reach.

"Come on, guys, settle down." Sophia clapped her hands and managed to wrangle their attention. "Ms. Hart's going to talk about lighting today." She took the chair behind her desk and motioned for Hannah to start.

Abby's eyes lit with anticipation from her seat

in the front row, and Hannah smiled at her as she began her presentation. "Everyone knows lighting in photography is important. But sometimes too much light can actually be a bad thing." Hannah held up a sample shot, where the flash had washed out the entire picture.

Abby sat on the edge of her seat, eyes following Hannah's every move and drinking in each photograph as she went on. Too bad the rest of the kids weren't as interested, though as Sophia had said, there was a definite change from Monday. At least they gave each photo Hannah passed around the room a cursory glance.

"Last week, Abby asked a question about lighting when taking a picture with a phone camera." Hannah collected the last of the pictures that had been passed around and slid them back in their protective folder, then pulled the handouts she'd prepared from an envelope. "I've made you all a list of tips to practice when you go home. Next week let me know if you think you took better pictures based on this advice." The kids accepted the handout, several of them looking longingly at their backpacks or purses where their phones nestled, turned off via school rules.

Sophia stood and pulled her own phone from her purse. "How about we take a few shots now with my phone and we can put Ms. Hart's guidelines into practice." The kids cheered, all vying to be first.

A knock sounded on the closed door a moment before it opened. Hannah looked up as Jude stepped inside, and her earlier hesitations flooded her body in full force. She took a deep breath and tried to keep a natural smile on her face. Maybe if she ignored the awkward conversation from Monday, he would, too.

Although it'd be a lot easier to ignore him if he didn't look so good in that gray pinstriped suit.

"Sorry to interrupt," he called above the din of the students chattering excitedly as Sophia divided them into groups of four. "I was hoping to speak with Ms. Hart before my three o'clock meeting."

Hannah's heart stammered in her chest. Her? Why? Sophia shot her a puzzled look, appearing equally confused, but gestured for her to go ahead. "I'll handle this. We'll show you what we've accomplished when you get back."

Hannah reluctantly met Jude in the deserted hallway, keeping her eyes down and feeling way too much like a student in trouble. The door clicked shut softly behind her and she crossed her arms, waiting for him to speak first. With her luck, she'd unknowingly offend him again. She didn't want to get on the school administration's bad side, especially when she wasn't even a certified teacher. When the students had started actually growing interested in what she'd taught today, something shifted inside her. She didn't just want to teach them—she *needed* to. Needed to feel productive, needed to feel like she was making a difference.

Needed to be needed.

"You look like Terrence McAllister did when I busted him last week for sneaking off campus." Jude shook his head with a smile that slowly relaxed Hannah's stiff position. "Am I that intimidating?"

She couldn't help but offer a small smile in return. "Maybe it's the suit."

He laughed, the husky sound melting the last of her nerves. "I'll be sure to have a word with my tailor." His grin faded at the corners, and his deep blue eyes took on a serious sheen. "I'm sorry I made you uneasy the other day. I let a personal matter affect my reaction to your generous offer, and I apologize."

Such formal wording—was that how he always spoke, or was that something he hid behind? Would be interesting to find out, to get to know him well enough to discover his quirks.

She certainly had enough of her own.

But then again, did she really want to get to know someone like Jude better, someone she could apparently offend so easily and never understand why? He'd apologized, so maybe it hadn't been her fault after all. Maybe he just didn't like receiving something—even something like photography services—free. A lot of men would take that as a slam on their pride. Still…

Hannah waited for more details, but he didn't offer them, leaving her with only more questions. She rescued them both from the silence that was inching toward awkward. "I guess we've all been there at one point or another. I'm sorry if I offended you."

"No, it was my fault alone." Jude shifted positions, casually resting his weight against the tiled wall. The motion sent an enticing wave of spicy cologne Hannah's way, weakening her knees. Pathetic. Had it been that long since she'd been in close proximity to a man?

Actually, yes. Sad, but true. Hannah bit her lower lip. She shouldn't go there. It would accomplish nothing. Jude was trying to right a wrong, nothing more. No way did he feel the attraction that threatened to level Hannah's legs out from under her.

Not when she looked the way she did.

"I've been concerned about a school issue, and the stress from— Well, I overreacted. No excuses." Jude hesitated and Hannah looked up, searching his gaze, eager to see his secrets but not sure why it mattered so much.

She looked away as a rush of warmth heated her stomach. Though she wasn't on the payroll, Jude was still an authority figure, and she had no business teasing herself with what would surely be a dead end. If only... But no, she couldn't go back down that road. She'd traveled it enough in the months after her car accident.

"Thanks for saying so." She drew a deep breath, forcing herself to meet his gaze briefly before pretending great interest in the bulletin board on the wall. Then she realized she'd provided him with a full view of her scarred cheek, and she quickly turned the opposite way.

Jude's gaze followed her motion, and a flush rode an unwelcome passage up Hannah's neck. Definitely a one-sided attraction. He had no reason to be drawn to her, and a jagged, three-inch reason not to.

Hannah straightened her shoulders, determined not to let him see her vulnerabilities. It would get them nowhere. "If that's all, I better get back to the class." A roar of laughter burst from inside the classroom, and Hannah took that as her cue. She reached for the knob, and Jude held out one hand as if to stop her before letting it drop back to his side. The traitorous blush claimed new real estate on her neck and chest and she forced herself not to look away, to hold her ground. She had nothing to be embarrassed about.

Unless he could read her mind.

Head tilted, Jude's eyes searched hers before resignation released her from their navy blue hold. "All right. Then I guess I'll see you around."

Hannah nodded once before slipping back inside the classroom.

Not if she could help it.

Chapter Three

A gust of October wind sent myriad crimson and gold leaves skittering past Hannah's feet. She adjusted the settings on her Nikon and squinted through the viewfinder. Perfect. As soon as her eleven o'clock appointment arrived at the park, she'd set the siblings up on the low branches of this oak and be able to catch the last of the morning light.

A car door slammed from the lot behind her, and Hannah turned in time to see what had to be the McDuffy family rushing toward her. The teenage girl, Sarah, if she remembered correctly, held her hands up to protect her spiral-curled hair from the wind, while the younger boy—Adam?—hurried toward her, carefree. Hannah waved and smiled, never tired of seeing what a few years in age and gender could mean for priorities.

A second girl hurried behind the first, and once they cleared the shadow of the pavilion, Hannah blinked. Abby. But not the braided, plaid Abby. This one had on subtle makeup and was dressed more like her friend in trendy jeans and a sparkly layered top.

"Hey, guys." Hannah smiled. "Abby, I didn't expect to see you here!"

"You know Ms. Hart?" Mrs. McDuffy asked in surprise.

Abby nodded, avoiding her gaze. Hannah frowned. That wasn't like her. She was so personable in class.

"The girls had a sleepover last night and thought it'd be fun if Abby tagged along." Mrs. McDuffy tried in vain to smooth her son's cowlick. "Oh, well. I guess photography is meant to record accuracy anyway."

"Don't worry. I can do wonders with editing." Hannah winked. "Come on, guys, I thought we'd take a few shots in this tree over here."

"Cool!" Adam bolted forward, scrambling for the lowest branch.

Sarah wrinkled her nose and stared at the tree like it might spring to life and devour her. "Will I get dirty?"

"I have tissues in my bag." Hannah urged her forward. Mrs. McDuffy strolled a few paces back to lean against the fence separating the park from the road. But Abby stood awkwardly next to Hannah, head still turned down, feigning great interest in her shoes. Hannah took a quick shot of

Sarah and Adam in the tree. "Adam, scoot closer toward the trunk." She waited while he shifted, lowering her voice. "You okay, Abby?"

"Uh-huh." The breeze nearly carried away the soft reply, and Hannah wondered if she should press the issue or take the girl's cue and leave it alone. She never liked being pushed to talk about things when she was younger. Best to ignore it for now—maybe distraction would open her up.

"Adam, that's perfect." Hannah took a few more shots then tilted her head. "Sarah, can you stand on the lowest branch? Adam, sit on the one above her." The kids scrambled to follow orders, Sarah pausing twice to wipe her hands.

Hannah dropped to her stomach, laying flat on the ground, to catch a unique angle.

Abby gaped at her. "You don't mind getting dirty?"

"Nope. That's why I wear old clothes to photo shoots." Hannah rolled sideways and braced her arm on her knee to get a sideways shot of the kids grinning through the leaves. "Thanks, guys! Let's take a few by the slides." She slowed her pace to match Abby's as the siblings and Mrs. McDuffy headed toward the playground equipment. The wind lifted Abby's blond hair, flowing freely across her shoulders, and turned the strands to honey. "Speaking of clothes, you look cute today. Trying out a new look?"

Abby looked over her shoulder, and then lowered her voice even though no one was around. "It's only for fun. I don't get to wear it often."

Hannah hiked her bag higher on her shoulder. "Why not? You look great."

"My dad likes my other look better." She rolled her eyes. "You know, the baby look with ponytails and dresses."

"I see." But she didn't, really. Hannah could understand a father being overprotective with his daughter—after all, her daddy was the same way even though she was almost thirty and lived three states away—but it wasn't as if Abby was doing anything inappropriate. However, these early teen years were rough, and on a single parent, probably rougher than she realized. "For what it's worth, you're a pretty girl either way."

A pleased blush tinted Abby's cheeks and she smiled shyly. "Thanks, Ms. Hart." As if a burden were suddenly lifted, she waved her arm at Sarah several paces ahead. "Hey, wait up!"

Hannah watched Abby jog across the park, glad the girl's smile was firmly back in place. She couldn't help but wonder about Abby's mom. Had she died? Had she and Jude divorced? He carried a burden in his eyes that resembled grief, so maybe an accident had stolen the former Mrs. Bradley. It seemed so unfair that such a sweet girl like Abby, in need of female guidance, would be robbed of her mother. Hannah's hand went to the scar on her face, her fingers tracing the slightly curved pattern she could draw in her sleep. But life wasn't fair—she was walking proof of that.

Enough bitterness. Hannah joined the group on the slides and placed the kids in different positions on the equipment. "Adam, tone back the smile a bit, okay?" The boy's toothy grin held more cheese than a warehouse in Wisconsin. She nodded as he narrowed his smile to something more natural. "Sarah, your necklace is crooked. Now, everyone say 'school's out'!"

The kids laughed on cue and Hannah took the shot.

After several more pictures, Mrs. McDuffy suggested that Abby get on the top of the jungle gym beside Sarah. "I think a few friend photos are in order."

Hannah hesitated. Jude had made it clear he didn't want any free photography, but if this was Mrs. McDuffy's idea—and money—then why would he resist? Technically, it wouldn't be free at all.

Decision made, Hannah nodded. "Sure thing." She crouched at the end of the slide, attempting to capture on camera the friendship that shone so sincerely in real life between the girls. Linking arms, they slid down the slide. *Click.* She caught them posing on the wooden bridge connecting two jungle gyms. *Click.* And again on the swings, legs pumping furiously as if they were children instead of almost teenagers.

Hannah paused to study the photos on her camera's LCD screen, admiring the innocence and beauty in both of their faces. A particular photo caught Hannah's eyes, and she looked up at Abby, then glanced back at her camera, grinning as an idea took root. Just because Hannah needed to keep her distance from the handsome assistant principal didn't mean she couldn't take an opportunity to help mend a fence between father and daughter.

And she knew just how to do it.

Jude frowned at the budget on his desk, wishing the numbers would rearrange themselves into something presentable. This wasn't looking good—in fact, it was getting downright grim. He shoved the papers away with a sigh, wishing it was as easy to push aside the stress headache now permanently taking up residence in his neck. Head Principal Coleman had sent another email to the upper staff today, clarifying that the electives at school were in danger because of the budget and there would be big decisions to make in the near future. Exactly what that meant, Jude had yet to discover.

Part of him didn't even want to know.

Jude sighed. Between Abby's teenage pride and this issue with the budget, he rarely had a moment's peace. He rolled a pencil between his fingers, staring at the yellow blur flipping over his knuckles. It didn't help that thoughts of Hannah consumed him more than they should have over the weekend. With Abby spending the night at a friend's house, he had ample time to wonder what he said wrong in his apology Friday afternoon. Though Hannah's words assured him all was well, her expression and manner had certainly not as she excused herself to go back to the class. Was she still offended? Or simply cautious?

It shouldn't matter. Even if his attraction to her was obvious—though hopefully not obvious to *her*—he had to tamp it down. He had no business with a photographer, no interest in being with someone who constantly reminded him of everything he was attempting to keep his daughter from.

He groaned. It figured. An attractive woman finally snagged his interest, without the help of Abby's inevitable matchmaking attempts, but he couldn't—make that wouldn't—pursue it. It wouldn't be fair, not until he figured a few things out about himself, first—assuming he ever did.

Jude's secretary, Mrs. Oakes, tapped on his open door, her frizzy dark hair even more out of place today than usual. He winced, knowing her stress was partly a consequence of his own. He made a mental note to take full advantage of the upcoming secretary appreciation day.

"Sir, Ms. Hart is here to see you."

Hannah? All thoughts of secretary appreciation fled his mind. Despite logic warning him otherwise, Jude's heart hammered a telltale thump and he dropped the pencil still in his hand. "Great.

Send her in." Maybe he could practice being a professional in front of her now, rather than nearly moony as he'd been during their hallway talk—though not as easily done as said. It wasn't just her appearance that knocked Jude off center. After all, he'd been around attractive women before—had married one, for that matter—but rather something deeper. Something about Hannah seemed to look right through him and see things he didn't show very often.

Make that ever.

How did she get under his skin like that? Maybe he was more desperate for female company than he'd realized. Maybe it *was* time to date again, if only to keep these crazy thoughts at bay when around Hannah.

Because he sure couldn't date her.

Hannah appeared in the door frame seconds later, her shoulder-length brown hair swept up on one side with a clip, revealing the long line of her neck above the scoop of her sweater. He cleared his throat, hoping she hadn't caught him staring. Even with the scar slightly hidden under the curtain of hair on her left side, she was beautiful.

"Hi." She hesitated in the doorway, clutching a manila envelope and looking as timid as his students did when they came to his office. "Is this a good time?"

"Of course." He motioned to the hard plastic seat in front of his desk where many a student had pouted, cried, yelled, or all of the above, and waited until Hannah sat before doing the same. "Sorry that chair is so uncomfortable. Usually the people sitting in it are in trouble."

"Then it's the perfect way to start their punishment." Hannah shifted in the seat and Jude couldn't help but laugh.

"How can I help you today, Hannah?" He liked saying her name. Too much. *Rein it in.* No point in sending mixed messages, messages he couldn't act on.

Even though too much of him already wanted to.

She opened the envelope she held with manicured fingers, and Jude's relaxed smile faded to a slight frown. Miranda had been adamant about her weekly manicures and pedicures during their short marriage, a fact that had put their barely existent young family budget on a strain. But she argued that if she was going to have a baby and ruin her body, she should get to have pretty nails. He'd agreed with her at the time. But after she lost her baby weight and ended up a size smaller than she'd started out being, he knew he was in trouble—and that trouble had nothing to do with spending two hundred dollars a month on nail care.

Now he wished women would just go back to nail-biting.

Hannah pulled an eight-by-ten-size sheet from the envelope, and from the quick glimpse he got before she hid it from his view, he gathered it was a picture. "I know you said you weren't interested in having a session done, but since Abby tagged along to her friend's session this past weekend, they suggested the idea of friend photos. I thought you'd like to have this one." She slowly turned the picture so he could see.

His breath caught at the sight of his daughter, a close-up of her beaming from the top of a slide, head tilted back and hair naturally highlighted in the sun. Jude reached across the desk and took the photo Hannah offered, his stomach a hard knot. Abby looked beautiful—of course. Like she had a choice with her mom's portion of genes in her. He licked his lips, wishing the rock now lodged in his throat would settle back down in his stomach.

Nodding once, he cleared his throat. "Thank you. This is thoughtful." Surely Hannah didn't intend the knifelike wound twisting his insides. Despite that, he did like the picture. Because of his own memories and fears, he hadn't taken nearly enough pictures of his daughter growing up. But if he did, and displayed them around the house, she would see how gorgeous she was and get the same idea Miranda had. He couldn't lose his daughter the same way he lost his wife.

He refused to let her travel that path of destruction.

"I'm so glad you like it." Hannah sat back in her chair, exhaling with a smile. She balanced the envelope on her lap. "I took a few more. But that one was my favorite."

His eyes darted back to the print. It *was* a great shot. But…wait a minute. Abby's hair was down and loose, which was unusual. And her clothes— he squinted, certain his eyes were playing tricks on him. What was she wearing? That shirt was not something he'd purchased. Neither was the makeup.

His fingers tightened on the photo and he quickly dropped it on his desk before he could crinkle the fragile paper. In fact, Abby hadn't even told him she was going with her friend to a photo shoot at all. How many other lies lingered between them?

Hannah's eyebrows knitted together, as if reading his mind. Or maybe he was just that obvious these days. "What's wrong?"

"This is— She knows better than to—" Jude cut off his own sentence and pinched the bridge of his nose, uncertain how much to reveal to Hannah but unable to keep the frustration from bubbling up and over. "She's wearing makeup. And clothes I don't allow. She lied to me."

Hannah's face paled. "Lied? I knew she looked different than usual, more trendy, but I never thought—"

"She knows the rules." Abby was his kid. And his kid and trendy didn't mix. Not that Hannah could understand that.

Hannah held up both hands in defense. "I'm sorry. I didn't mean to open a can of worms here. Mrs. McDuffy suggested the group photo and—" She reached for the picture on his desk as if to take it back, but Jude placed one hand on it and held it in place.

"Leave it."

She leaned back, confusion splayed across her face. "I was hoping to surprise you in a good way, not get Abby in trouble."

"You didn't know. She did." Jude sighed, reminding himself this wasn't Hannah's fault. It was Abby's. Why couldn't she accept no for an answer and trust him as her father? Whether his instincts were right or wrong, she'd disobeyed.

And now he had proof.

"I'll keep this. I do appreciate the gesture. It's just…complicated."

Hannah stood, frowning, her fingers tapping the envelope pressed against her leg. She opened her mouth, then closed it before doing the same again twice.

Jude recognized the hesitation from his students, the desire to say what was on their mind but being afraid of getting in trouble if they did. He was tired of beating around the bush. He wanted honesty. Craved it, especially after the way his own daughter evaded him. "Go ahead. You won't offend me."

Hopefully. Not offending Jude seemed to be getting harder to accomplish lately. Was that why

Abby had been at odds with him so much the past several months? He thought he'd gotten a handle on his temper in the counseling sessions he attended after Miranda's desertion years ago, then again after receiving news of her death. Maybe it was the stress of the budget wearing on him. That alone was enough to drive a man crazy, much less this drama with his almost-teenager.

At Hannah's hesitation, he pressed on. "Please, say what's on your mind."

Her words rushed out, tumbling over each other like a waterfall off a cliff. "I know I'm not a parent, but I'm curious why you have these rules for Abby. She's a good kid. I know you know that. But honestly, she looked cute at the park. Not inappropriate by any means."

Jude stood, his irritation now welling despite his good intentions to tamp it down. He'd heard enough about his parenting ability from both his parents and his in-laws. He didn't need it from a stranger, too—even one as sweet and attractive as Hannah. She didn't know what she was talking about, didn't know him or his family. He pressed his lips into a thin line. "You're right. You're not a parent. So you can't understand this."

Her eyes widened and she flinched as if he'd dealt a physical blow. Her jaw clenched, and she nodded once, her voice soft. "Then I'm sorry to interfere." She glanced at the envelope in her hands, and with a flick of her wrist, tossed the entire package on top of his desk.

Guilt rocked Jude's senses as several different-size photos of the same image slipped free of the envelope. Once again, he was taking his frustration out on the wrong person. Jude held out his hand. "Hannah, wait. I shouldn't have—"

Without looking back, Hannah slipped out of the room.

Chapter Four

With a temper like that, the man should've been a pro wrestler, not an assistant principal.

Hannah fumed the entire time it took her to stalk from Jude's office to Sophia's classroom, which wasn't long considering her strides were peppered with indignation. What happened? How could one picture, hinting of loose hair and a tube of lip gloss, set off a polished professional like Jude? It didn't make sense. He'd originally seemed fine with the photograph—pleased, even.

Until the switch flipped and it was out with Dr. Jekyll, in with Mr. Hyde.

Hannah didn't have to be a math teacher to know something didn't add up. Jude's vibe toward Abby went beyond mere overprotective. He had a secret.

She knew because she had her own.

She paced outside Sophia's classroom, not ready to go inside until her blood pressure lowered. The dirt-streaked floor passed in a blur as she walked and turned, walked and turned. Jude had every right to raise his daughter the way he chose to, but this was ridiculous. The photo shoot had been done in complete innocence.

Hannah kept pacing, the bulletin board outside Sophia's classroom a kaleidoscope of blue and yellow construction paper in her peripheral vision. Maybe she should have stayed out of it, but how could she have turned Mrs. McDuffy down over something so trivial? And why would someone refuse a photo of their kid? A gorgeous photo, at that—not a boast of Hannah's talent, but of Abby's natural beauty. Hannah had barely even opened the picture in Photoshop. In fact, the only thing she'd done was enhance the lighting of the background. She hadn't touched Abby's direct image.

How could that make a father upset instead of proud?

Even now Jude's words echoed harshly in her mind. *You're right—you're not a parent.* He didn't know—couldn't know—how badly that hurt. The words themselves were an agreement, truthful. The average woman wouldn't have even flinched.

Yet here Hannah was stuck trying to remove a hundred stinging barbs from her heart.

"Hannah, what are you doing in the hallway?" Sophia poked her head outside her class, bracing one arm on the door frame. Her dozen colored bangles clanged together on her wrist, jerking Hannah from her ponderings.

She turned to face her friend. "Trying to figure out why men do what they do."

Sophia's eyebrows rose. "Oh, honey, you better come on in. That one will take you until the end of the semester. Maybe longer." She tugged Hannah inside. "What happened?"

Hannah nibbled her lower lip as they both leaned against the side of Sophia's cluttered desk. "I think I made a mistake." Logic began a slow descent, replacing the initial burst of frustration. "You remember last week Jude said he didn't want me to take pictures of Abby for my portfolio?"

Sophia crossed her arms, bracelets jingling. "Yeah…" Her voice trailed off into a wary question.

"I did anyway, though it wasn't my initial idea." Hannah let out a long breath as she filled Sophia in on the photo shoot from Saturday and her conversation with Jude. "I honestly thought he just didn't want to accept anything free, so I believed having it on Mrs. McDuffy's account would skirt the issue. It wasn't a free session I did as a favor that way, you know? But now I think he has other reasons."

"Jude's always been very careful with Abby," Sophia agreed, moving to the chalkboard to erase her previous class's bulletin points. "But this seems like overkill, even for him. Maybe he's upset that she disobeyed his rules. He could have been projecting that anger onto you."

Hannah coughed as a wave of chalk dust drifted toward her. "If so, it seems to be a new habit of his."

It wouldn't continue to be a habit. After today, she couldn't imagine either of them finding anything agreeable to talk about. Two people who constantly offended the other had no reason to be around each other. Authority figure or not.

Students began filing into the room, and Hannah shot Sophia a look, silently agreeing to finish the conversation later.

As Abby took her seat in the front row, eyes sparkling with anticipation, a twinge of guilt flitted through Hannah's stomach. She'd inadvertently caused trouble for the young girl. It seemed only fair to warn Abby of what she would face after school.

"Abby, do you mind staying a minute?" Hannah kept her voice low so the other students wouldn't hear her request and assume the girl had done something wrong. Sophia had excused herself after dismissing the class, allowing Hannah space to have their pending conversation—and they'd have to hurry, since Jude was surely used to Abby meeting him directly after school.

Abby looked up from packing her backpack and offered an unsure smile. "Sure, Ms. Hart." She zipped the bag and tucked the straps around her shoulders. "What's up?"

Hannah sat on top of the desk across from Abby's. "There's something you should know." This wouldn't be easy. The rock that settled in Hannah's stomach seemed proof enough of that. She swallowed, wishing she'd minded her own business from the start and not put either of them in this position.

"What is it?" Abby picked at a star sticker she'd put on the top of her otherwise bare hand. No chipped fingernail polish coated her nails, no rings sparkled on her fingers, no bracelets bunched at her wrist like almost every other girl in the class. Abby obviously knew she was different, or she wouldn't have deliberately broken her dad's rules to try to fit in.

Hannah could relate to being left out. Maybe she hadn't felt that way as a teenager, but as a woman, it still wasn't easy. The stares, the instant flickering of eyes from her own gaze to her cheek. The curiosity lingering in people's voices, hinting at the question no one dared to ask.

No—never easy.

A wave of compassion washed over Hannah, and she leaned forward, coaxing the younger girl to meet her gaze. At least Abby's struggles were superficial instead of permanent, as easily removed in the time it took to change clothes or untie a braided plait of hair. But as far Jude was concerned, Abby didn't necessarily have those choices.

"You know those pictures I took at the park?"

"Yeah?" Abby cleared her throat. "I mean, yes, ma'am."

Hannah briefly closed her eyes. Such manners on such a sweet girl—why on earth was Jude so particular about her appearance? It didn't make sense.

Hannah forced a smile. "Some of them really turned out well, and I ended up making a few copies for you."

Abby nodded, even as her gaze turned questioning, guarded, as if she could see what was coming.

Hannah shifted positions on the desk. Man, she hated being in the middle of this. Abby's deception should have stayed between her and her dad, and if Hannah hadn't had gotten involved with that silly picture, she wouldn't be sending the girl off to the parental guillotine.

She drew a deep breath before continuing. The moment of the truth. "I gave one to your dad before class."

All the blood drained from Abby's face and she stumbled backward a step. "You did?" Panic highlighted her delicate features, and she bit down so hard on her lip Hannah halfway expected to see blood. "Was he—was he mad?"

"He was…surprised." Hannah chose her words carefully, then sighed. No more lies; that's what got Abby into this mess in the first mess. "But yes. He seemed upset—mostly because you snuck around.

He seemed to think you know better than to wear makeup without permission."

Abby closed her eyes briefly. "I know I shouldn't have." Then she locked her gaze with Hannah's, eyes shiny with pending tears. "But I'm so tired of being a baby."

Abby's heartfelt admission tore at Jude's heart, and he rested his forehead against the door frame of Sophia's classroom, allowing the cool metal plating to calm his temper. He'd hurried to meet Abby after the final bell, ready to walk her straight to the car so he could dole out a much-pondered punishment for her deception over last weekend.

Until her confession pierced his conscience.

Was he pushing her so hard in the opposite direction of her mother that she'd eventually come full circle around the other side?

Jude's stomach clenched, and he eased away from the door. Hannah shouldn't have warned Abby about his discovery, though he guessed in Hannah's shoes he'd have felt guilty, too. Still, did anyone trust him to do things his way for his own daughter?

Maybe his dream of having a big family needed to die. He already struggled to be a good father to the kid he had. Still, growing up as an only child hadn't been fun. He wanted Abby to have siblings, to be a part of a big family unit she could feel safe in, rely on. Her childhood had been sketchy enough—she deserved stability. Love. Loyalty. It was already too late for a sibling to be close enough in age for her to play with, but she could easily take on the role of protector for them one day. Teach them things, show them the ropes of life.

Assuming Jude didn't let her fall along the way.

A student hurrying down the hall, probably hoping to catch their bus, scurried past Jude, reminding him he shouldn't be standing in the hallway imagining things that probably would never happen. He took a step toward the door, then hesitated, Abby's distressed voice ringing in his ears. She'd been wrong to lie, but he wouldn't embarrass her further by openly admitting he'd overheard her private conversation with Hannah. He'd back up a few steps and clomp in that direction so they'd have warning.

But Hannah's soft response stopped him so fast, his loafer squeaked against the linoleum.

"Looking a little different doesn't make you a baby." Her gentle voice carried through the quietness of the now deserted hallway. "Besides, no matter what you wear or what you paint on your face, you're a beautiful girl."

A warning bell dinged in the back of Jude's mind. Abby didn't need frequent reminders of her appearance. Jude knew—from common sense, and from the dozens of parenting books thrust his way in the aftermath of his wife's desertion—the importance of showing his daughter her worth. But he wouldn't do that through overly praising her outward appearance and putting ideas in her head of how to abuse that beauty. She had to already know how stunning she was, anyway. Any daughter of Miranda's had no choice to be otherwise. She didn't need confirmation.

"I am?" Abby's voice sounded so tiny Jude almost missed it. A fist landed in his stomach and he sucked in a hard breath. She honestly didn't know? Impossible. But Abby wasn't the type to beg for compliments. Beg for attention, maybe, or beg to get her own way—never for praise. He'd made sure of that growing up.

Sudden uncertainty gnawed a hole in Jude's heart. Had he made sure of too much?

"Of course you are!" Hannah sounded as surprised as Jude felt. "Makeup wouldn't change that one bit. What's important is what's on the inside." She paused. "And disobeying your father is pretty ugly."

"I guess I never thought of it that way."

Jude risked a peek around the door frame, just enough to catch Abby absently scuffing the toe of her shoe against the floor. She wasn't making eye contact with Hannah, but she was listening.

That was a whole lot further than he'd ever gotten with her.

Why did Abby push him away, yet take the same exact advice from a near stranger? The woman factor must play a bigger part than he realized. Jude ducked back around the corner and ran one hand over his hair, the gelled strands sliding through his fingers. Abby needed an older friend, some sort of constant female presence in her life. Someone to do the girl-talk thing, someone to give a viewpoint on life and morals that wasn't his own repeating, broken record.

She needed a mom.

The thought broke a cold sweat on the back of Jude's neck.

He didn't want to be alone his entire life, and he truly wanted Abby to have sisters and brothers one day.

But out of all the women he'd casually dated over the past few years, there hadn't been a single one who'd ever come close to prompting thoughts of marriage. Or, for that matter, there'd never been one whom Abby looked at as she'd looked at Hannah—with respect. Sincerity. Admiration.

The exact same things Jude saw in Hannah, despite his lingering aggravation at her interference.

Jude rubbed a hand down his jaw. Apparently the budget stress was affecting him worse than he'd thought. Marriage and Hannah in the same sentence? He'd barely met the woman, and already they'd offended each other twice. He'd seen the look on her face when she stormed out of his office—in the week they'd known each other, he'd given her more reasons to laugh at him than accept an offer of a date. No, that was out of the question.

Jude licked his suddenly dry lips, a rare sense of panic seeping into his soul as Hannah's soft spoken clarifications of real beauty continued. She definitely had a handle on the concept of beauty that Miranda never had. But he needed to break up the little union forming inside before things got heavier, before Abby got even more attached.

Or before he did the same.

Chapter Five

Heavy footsteps preceded Jude into the classroom. Hannah hopped off the desk as if she were a student getting busted. She knew it'd be a matter of time until he showed up, but she still couldn't help the twinge of sympathy as Abby's face fell. The younger girl turned slowly to face her fate, head up, gaze down.

But Jude wasn't looking at Abby.

"How was class?" He smiled at Hannah, casually—too casually.

She narrowed her eyes. Had he been listening outside the door? She crossed her arms over her chest, immediately defensive although he had every right to hear conversations about his daughter—in his school. Would he be mad she'd warned Abby about the photo? Or had he expected it?

"Class was great." She had to be honest, even though saying something positive at the moment felt a little like losing whatever this weird battle was she'd found herself fighting.

Jude shoved his hands in his pants pockets and nodded slowly. "Always good to…hear." A slight smirk lit his eyes as Hannah's gaze jerked to meet his. Her neck flushed with heat. He'd listened, all right.

Enough of the games. "I better get going. I have a photo shoot to prepare for tomorrow." Hannah shouldered her bag and offered Abby, who'd been silent during the entire exchange, an encouraging smile. "See you later this week."

"Who's your client?" Jude shifted his weight, resting against the side of Abby's desk as if he had no cares in the world, no punishments to dole out, no points to prove.

No apologies to make.

Though on second thought, Hannah owed him one for her involvement in the first place. Best to call it even and move on.

But she couldn't tear her eyes away from his arresting blue gaze.

"It's an engagement shoot." She had to look away during the word *engagement*. Even now, the thought of photographing the happy, smiling couple tomorrow tied her stomach in knots. Engagement shoots were always tough. Young people blissfully naive of the future, unaware of the way life could change in a single second, in the time it took for a drunk driver to run a red light. They believed everything would always be the way they'd planned—and why shouldn't they? They had no reason to think otherwise.

No daily scars to remind them how deeply dreams were crushed.

"Are you free afterward?"

Jude's voice ripped Hannah away from the past, leaving her gaping in the present. She opened her mouth, but words escaped her. Why in the world did Jude care what she did tomorrow? It wasn't like he wanted to schedule his own photo shoot. And he wasn't asking her out...surely not.

Surprise flickered across Jude's expression, as if he startled even himself by the sudden question. But he squared his shoulders and repeated the shocking words. "Are you free afterward? I'd like to buy you a cup of coffee."

Hannah's breath hitched. Coffee? With Jude? Alone? She could think of about a dozen reasons to say no.

And maybe only one reason to say yes.

Abby looked between Hannah and her dad, confusion pinching her eyebrows. "What about me?"

"You're going to be grounded." Jude frowned, as if finally remembering why he even came to hunt Abby down in the first place. "So you'll be doing homework while we're out." He lifted his gaze back to Hannah. "That is, if Ms. Hart agrees to go."

"I—I…" Hannah's voice trailed off, and she clutched at the necklace around her throat, desperate to hide the blush she couldn't control that she knew by now had to be lighting her scar like a beacon. She tilted her head so her hair covered her left cheek, and nibbled on her lower lip. "I can't."

Abby released the breath she'd obviously been holding, and her shoulders slumped. Hannah knew the feeling. It almost hurt to say no. But what good could come from a coffee—dare she say date?—with Jude? For a moment, she'd wanted to entertain the idea that his quick temper and snappiness somehow stemmed from a connection with her, from a place he fought deep inside just as she did. That maybe he really did want to take her out, get to know her, see the real her beneath the pretension—and the scars.

But that was asking a lot of a man she'd known for a week, who at the moment had more reasons to fire her than take her on a date.

Jude must have seen Abby's disappointment, too. "Abby, please go wait in the car."

"But, Dad—"

"You're not really in a position to argue here, honey." Jude's voice, gentle but firm, allowed no argument.

With a humble nod, Abby took the keys Jude handed her and scurried out of the room.

"You trust her with your keys?" Hannah couldn't

help her tone, couldn't hold back the rest of the sentence that flitted between them, unspoken yet incredibly clear. *But not with designer jeans and a little bit of makeup?*

The hum of the fluorescent light above filled the silence, until Jude stepped a few feet closer, leaning against the student's desk beside hers. "Abby's a good kid."

Hannah bit back the *I know* that threatened to pour out, and restrained herself to a nod as she crossed her arms, determined to listen without judgment.

Or at least without as *much* judgment. Handsome or not, the man remained a puzzle—especially when it came to all things Abby. How could someone who cared so much be so hard-nosed?

"I know there are rumors." A muscle clenched in Jude's jaw, and he looked down briefly, flicking a piece of lint off the leg of his slacks. "I don't know if you believe them."

The statement turned into a question. Hannah shrugged, her heart climbing in her throat. "I don't see why it matters what I think." Flashes of their previous conversation in his office danced before her, and she straightened her shoulders, her resolve about saying no strengthened. "You actually made it quite clear that it doesn't."

"And I owe you an apology—hence the coffee." Jude offered a slight smile, one that set Hannah's insides trembling more than she wanted to admit.

"Besides, I overheard a little bit of what you told Abby. She really responds to you." Jude looked over his shoulder, as if he could somehow see Abby through the layers of brick and steel. "I'd hoped maybe you'd give me some pointers."

Jude's lips thinned, as if the very act of saying the words out loud pained him, but it had to be hard to ask for help—a single dad, attempting to prove to the world he could handle a preteen by himself. It couldn't be easy, and no matter how many times he lost his temper with her, Hannah admired him. Abby was obviously *his* responsibility—he hadn't pawned her off as she'd see dads do before. He cared—maybe too much about the wrong things, but again, that was her opinion. What mattered the most was Abby. If he wanted help with her, how could she say no? While Hannah couldn't fathom seeing Jude for any personal reasons, she could easily think of a sweet, blonde, blue-eyed reason to do just that.

"Okay." She smiled back, hoping her smile didn't shake as much as her hands did. "Coffee it is. I'll be free around seven."

They made plans to meet at a local shop not far from the school, and Jude rushed off to meet Abby at the car. Hannah packed up her camera bag, unsure what to do with the variety of emotions skittering inside. It wasn't a date—for either of them. More like it was a desperate dad needing advice on how to girl-talk with his kid. Hopefully

Hannah could help smooth things over for the mismatched father/daughter duo.

Without letting her heart get involved.

It was hard to concentrate on Monday night football when Jude spent more time replaying and analyzing his pathetic conversation with Hannah than the sports broadcasters did with the plays. Jude aimed the remote at the TV and clicked mute, successfully eliminating the monotone voices of the announcers but doing little to ease the thoughts that ricocheted through his head.

Something happened between the time he strolled inside the classroom, forcing a casual air as if he hadn't been listening at the door, determined to break up the duo forming inside—and the time he opened his mouth and heard the request for a coffee date fly from his lips. Something had happened, all right. Something like the aroma of Hannah's vanilla perfume teasing all logic from his senses. Something like the respect Abby was showing him for the first time in weeks.

Something like the idea of the three of them together.

He picked up his nearly empty cola and stared absently at the can. Crazy. He barely even knew Hannah, and here he was nudging into her life, picturing visions he had no right to imagine. But he did owe her an apology—his temper lately seemed more worthy of a pro wrestler than it did an assistant principal. He wasn't leaving a very good impression of his school, and regardless of the stress he was under, regardless of the way she'd interfered with his daughter, Hannah didn't deserve him behaving like he were in the ring.

God, when did I get like this? The prayer slipped through the cracks of the wall Jude erected some time ago, and he ran a hand over his rough jaw, in need of a shave. Miranda used to accuse him of being quick-tempered, but not like this. Never like this. He could see himself morphing into this person he didn't want to be. Even now, remembering Abby's lies and deceit sent his blood boiling a few degrees more than it should.

No wonder Miranda had chosen drugs and the high life over him.

Jude set his drink down and watched the commercial playing on the big screen with bleary eyes, wishing the headache roaring in the back of his head would stop—and take all the back and forth, wishy-washy contradictions over Hannah with it. No, he couldn't bring Hannah any further into his messed-up world. Coffee would be an apology. Nothing more. Jude didn't need to date an employee, even if she was a temp and not technically employed by the school. Nothing good could come from that. She'd be hanging around for a few weeks helping Sophia, and after all his blunders, he didn't need to make that time more awkward than it already would be. Then she'd be gone, and his problem would be over.

Besides, Hannah could never truly own the title of Ms. Right, even if Jude grew even more selfish than he already was and actually wanted her to claim it. She was a photographer—everything in her thrived on making things beautiful through that thick camera lens.

He refused to fight that kind of ugly again. He saw where it led, what it destroyed. Better to steer clear than to get sucked in, especially where Abby was concerned.

Jude clicked the remote control and abrupt sound from the next commercial flooded his living room. He inched the volume down, mindful of Abby trying to sleep across the hall, and closed his eyes, wishing he remembered how to pray. Wishing he could erase the last decade's worth of mistakes and choices.

"I have to admit, I've never heard of an engagement shoot taking place inside a skating rink." Sophia set Hannah's bag of props on the bench against the carpeted wall the next afternoon and sank down beside it.

Hannah held one finger to her lips, before waving to the young couple on the wooden rink a few yards away. "Lucy's on the local Derby team. And Mark is— Well, Mark's…"

"In love?" Sophia supplied, as Mark wobbled

helplessly on his skates. He would have fallen, if Lucy hadn't grabbed his arms. The couple laughed, the happy sound bubbling over the low brick wall separating them from Hannah.

"Apparently." Hannah shook her head, wondering what it would be like to be so committed to someone, you'd willingly embrace all their quirks—when it was obvious your interests vastly differed.

Mark attempted a slow circle on the floor with Lucy's help, their elbows linked and heads bent close together. Hannah nibbled on her lower lip. What did God have in store for this couple? Would they still be smiling a year after their wedding? Would they immediately have children?

Must be nice to have the option.

She shook off the familiar pattern of bitterness before it could grow too dark, and turned her attention back to her friend. "Anyway, thanks for coming to help. It shouldn't be too crazy though, since Lucy was able to reserve the rink for us to do this privately." The skating rink might be a little unconventional, but most of the time, unconventional made for the best pictures. This would be fun—if she kept her focus on the job at hand and quit coveting a younger couple's life.

Sophia pulled off her boots and slid her feet into a pair of skates that looked as if they hadn't seen the light of day in a decade. "It's no problem. I sort of owe you after all you've done for my class. Our first photography session with CREATE is tomorrow, don't forget." She bent and began tying the laces. "Man, I haven't skated in forever."

"Obviously." Hannah gestured to her scuffed skates. "I'm surprised those still fit."

"They were new—in college." Sophia smirked as she yanked the laces into a knot. "What, you're not going to take pictures while rolling around with us?"

"I sort of value my camera equipment too much to risk that." Not to mention Hannah had zero balance on skates as a child, and she figured that fact hadn't changed with lack of practice over the past fifteen years.

Sophia stood smoothly on her skates, just as Lucy let go of Mark on the rink. He immediately fell hard on one knee. Sophia winced. "Ouch. I hope you can edit out bruises."

"Trust me, my editing program at home does wonders." Hannah slipped the proper lens onto her camera. "I can fix frizzy hair, sweat—whatever the client wants."

"Sort of like how the magazine people do for their models, I guess." Sophia blew a strand of her hair out of her eye as she began inching toward the wooden floor. "Speaking of models, guess what I heard through the teachers' lounge gossip mill?"

Hannah pulled a bouquet of fresh wildflowers from her prop bag and followed Sophia onto the floor toward the couple. "It's really none of my business." She hated gossip, especially after seeing people talking about her, gesturing to their own faces and whispering, wondering what had happened behind raised hands instead of asking her outright. No, gossip was not her thing.

"Are you sure?" Sophia's voice was singsongy, as if her old skates were somehow bringing back her more immature college days. "It's about Jude."

Hannah paused, wishing that fact didn't change her opinion about gossip in general. Then she shook it off. "You guys ready?" She motioned for Lucy and Mark to come to their side of the rink, then drew a deep breath, lowering her voice. "Sophia, it's still none of my business."

Unfortunately. She had to admit, though, she was a little curious how in the world Sophia went from saying "speaking of models" to this revelation. Surely Jude didn't model on the side.

Though with his charm and those business suits...well, she'd certainly buy the catalog.

Sophia watched as Lucy turned back to help Mark wobble their way. "How is it not your business? You're going out with him for coffee tonight."

"Only to talk about Abby. It's not a date." But earlier she'd debated for a solid hour on what to wear, as if it were. Maybe it wasn't supposed to be a date, but it could turn that direction. Maybe Jude was using his daughter as a cover-up for wanting to get to know Hannah better. It could happen. Anything could happen.

"It's not really gossip, anyway, more like a new piece of that handsome puzzle." Sophia took the flowers from Hannah and gave them a sniff. "Turns out, his ex-wife used to be a model."

Any lingering hopes of Jude noticing Hannah over a white chocolate mocha crashed and burned in the bubbling pool that was now her stomach. As if on their own accord, Hannah's fingers reached up and touched her scar, her spirits plummeting. Anything could happen? Right. And maybe Mark would be ready to compete in a professional Derby bout tomorrow.

"A model, huh? Like, for Sears?" Hannah's voice cracked, and she cleared her throat.

Sophia fixed her with a look. "I think a little more exotic than that."

No wonder Abby was so gorgeous. Hannah's former thoughts rose up in a chorus of too-familiar tormenters, and laughed in her face. How could she have ever even briefly entertained the idea that a man like Jude, used to physical perfection, could be interested in someone like her?

That's not fair, Hannah. You barely even know him. Her conscience blared a warning that she was crossing an emotional threshold she had no business crossing. But her runaway thoughts wouldn't obey and corral. She might not know Jude well, but she knew his temper—she'd had a front-row seat to that show, twice now. And she knew he must pride himself on image, always looking so professional and keeping such a close eye on Abby's wardrobe.

Hannah's hands tightened around her camera. And she knew how much he loved his daughter.

It's just a scar. You're not a mutant. People have seen worse. Hannah ran through the mental checklist of notes she tried to tell herself in the mirror every day after the accident, but failed now as she did then. Maybe it was just a scar—but when compared to a model, she might as well be significantly deformed.

But why was she comparing anyway? Before Jude's coffee request, he'd given her no reason to ever think he was more than her unofficial boss. She needed to tone down the wishes welling up in her chest. Reality was reality. Her fiancé hadn't wanted her after the accident. Why would someone like Jude? Especially after he knew the rest of her story.

"Are you okay?" Sophia tapped Hannah's arm, yanking her away from the dark place that threatened to consume her. "Lucy said they were ready. Twice."

Hannah inhaled sharply. "Of course. Let's go." She forced a smile for her clients' sakes, and called instructions to Sophia. "Bring those flowers to this wall over here, will you?" She arranged Lucy and Mark in a smiling embrace at the end of the rink, forcing herself to work through the cloudy haze still fogging her mind.

"I don't have to actually skate, do I?" Mark's tone was light but his eyes wary. He held Lucy so tightly, Hannah wondered if she'd have to edit white knuckles from the photos.

"No, sweetie. You stand there and look nice." Lucy reached up and playfully patted his cheek, humor lighting her eyes along with more than a little pity.

Pity. A second fist pummeled Hannah's midsection and she nearly lost her grip on her camera. What if Jude felt sorry for her, and that's why he wanted to talk about Abby over coffee? Make it at least feel a little like a date, because he figured that was as good as it would get for her? The only thing she hated more than feeling second-class was being pitied. She'd had enough of that in the weeks after her accident to last a lifetime. Being babied brought out the immature nature in her, made her deserve it. She refused to go back to that period in time.

"I don't want to look stupid in the pictures." Worry seeped through the nonchalant charade Mark had worn the past hour, wrinkling his bushy eyebrows.

Hannah leveled a smile at him before taking a quick practice shot to check the lighting. *Click.* "Don't worry, guys. I'll make you *both* look like Derby pros." She offered a wink, hoping to lighten her own mood as well as Mark's. *Click.* Her voice muffled as she took another shot. "Trust me—I'm great at masking the truth."

Chapter Six

Hannah breezed inside the local coffee shop, silky dark hair blowing across her lightly pinked cheeks. Jude rose from his chair in the back corner and lifted one hand to catch her attention, his heart picking up its pace a little at her appearance.

She reached up to corral her hair as the door shut behind her, sealing out the wind. He waved again and Hannah finally saw him and smiled, but the expression didn't seem to quite match her eyes. She motioned toward the counter and held up one finger, as if indicating she'd be over as soon as she ordered.

Jude had intended to buy the coffee for her, but she refused to look back in his direction. Rather than cause a scene by rushing to the counter, he sank slowly back into his chair, content to study Hannah from afar. Tension bunched her shoulders under the red sweater she wore with jeans. Casual—probably came from that photo shoot she'd mentioned yesterday. He stole a quick look down at his pressed dress shirt and slacks, a uniform he wore so often at school he rarely considered changing for other outings. Would he make Hannah uncomfortable being so dressed up?

Although, the distance in her expression as she made her way toward his table a few minutes later, coffee in hand, was already making him uncomfortable. What had he done? *He* was the one who was supposed to be distant tonight, holding back, making it clear this entire coffee meeting was about Abby. He didn't want to give the wrong impression.

But judging by Hannah's tight-lipped smile, one of them obviously already had.

He shifted in his seat. "Thanks for coming." The words sounded even more stilted out loud than they had in his head, and Jude berated himself as Hannah slid into the chair across from him. He tried again. "Seems pretty windy out."

That was worse. He shook his head slightly, determined not to speak again until Hannah did. Babbling niceties and commenting on the weather weren't helping. Maybe she'd had a stressful day.

He knew all about those.

"It's getting colder, too." Hannah shook her head so a curtain of hair covered her left cheek. Was that gesture a habit to her, or was she always that self-conscious about her scar? He wasn't a doctor by any means, but judging by its texture and color, the scar didn't appear to be very new.

Great, now he was staring. Jude looked away. This evening was definitely not going as planned. But then again, nothing seemed to go as planned lately.

He looked back, careful to meet Hannah's eyes, which narrowed as if she'd guessed the object of his previous perusal. "Colder, huh?" A chilly storm cloud sure seemed to hover over their table, which suddenly felt way too intimate back here in the corner, away from the hustle and bustle of patrons crowding the counter and the whir of blenders mixing up drinks. He cleared his throat, wishing he could clear away the awkwardness crowding them as easily. "How was your photo shoot?"

Hannah's eyes flickered with an undefined emotion. "It went well. I think the pictures will be unique." She let out a little laugh, one that still didn't ring quite sincere. "It was at a skating rink."

"That is different," Jude agreed. He and Miranda hadn't even taken professional engagement photos, had made do with his Polaroid in front of her parents' oak tree instead. He still hadn't been able to throw the picture away, though he'd held it next to a lighter more times than he could count, debating burning it to a crisp. It was the only picture he had of Miranda that he didn't mind looking at—and oh, there were plenty to choose from—back when her beauty was natural, her skin untouched by airbrushing, her tan from the sun instead of a bottle.

His gaze darted over Hannah's creamy complexion, which offered no hint of fake tan or plastic surgery. Was she caught up in image as so many women seemed to be or did she not care? By the way she hid her scar, she had to care some.

Jude averted his gaze and took a long sip of coffee. He had no business comparing Hannah to his ex-wife. Not only was it wrong, it was completely unnecessary—even if Hannah was coming out on top in many ways. He couldn't go there.

He set his cup down, searching for the professionalism that usually came so easily for him. Why did Hannah knock him off balance? He was a father, concerned about his daughter, and Hannah was simply his gateway into new communication with Abby. That was it.

Right. That was like saying the stout coffee in front of him would help him sleep tonight.

He tried to focus, get his head back in the game. "What kind of photo shoots do you do the most?" Somewhat of a dreaded topic for him, but at least now the conversational ball was in her court.

"I do a lot of engagements and weddings. But it seems like mostly kids these days. Parents are so eager to have their kids photographed." She shot him a pointed look over her mug. "Well, most of them."

So they were back to that. Jude's mouth dried,

and for the life of him, he couldn't think of anything else to say.

Hannah raised one eyebrow at him as she took a sip of her drink, apparently unwilling to help eliminate the awkward factor. In fact, he almost imagined she enjoyed seeing him struggle.

Time for a subject change. "So…about Abby."

"Right. Abby. The reason I'm here, apparently." Hannah tilted her chin up, her eyes meeting his in a challenge.

Game over. Jude leaned forward, unable to go on until he figured out what had her so uptight. "Hannah, did you have a bad day? Do you want to postpone this meeting?"

Her eyes darted to her cup before meeting his, and her gaze softened. "No, I'm sorry. It's—been a weird day. I really am here for Abby. Just like you are." She rolled in her lower lip, looking young and unsure. "What do you want to know?"

Truly, he wanted to know if she felt the same chemistry sizzling over the table between them as much as he did. But that wasn't the sort of question he could ask—or should, anyway. He hesitated, her instant lowering of defenses catching him off guard. He'd expected a little more fight from her before she gave in. But no, that was how *he* worked, not Hannah. Someone who *didn't* walk around with a ticking time bomb of a temper.

He let out a resigned sigh. "I'd like to talk about you first. About us."

Surprised pinched Hannah's expression. "What do you mean?"

Uh-oh. Now his feelings were jumping out his lips without a parachute. Jude clenched his coffee mug in both hands, warmth seeping through the blue ceramic. He tried to backtrack. "I meant, why we keep saying the wrong things."

"And doing them." Hannah offered a slight smile, one that looked as hopeless as he felt. "Like my taking pictures without your permission."

"And my blowing up at you for what must seem like no reason at all."

"I wasn't going to mention it, but…" Hannah's voice trailed off and a teasing spark lit her eyes.

This was the Hannah he had wanted to get to know better. Jude found himself relaxing before remembering his reservations. Why did he keep forgetting the emotional boundaries he'd anchored in place regarding this woman? She kept sneaking around them. First at school, when he invited her here, then in his thoughts, and even now, sitting across the table from him, a speck of whipped cream dotting the corner of her full lips.

Hannah tilted her head, her smile slowly fading. "You said what must *seem* like no reason…meaning you do have them."

"Did you think I was a bear without a cause?"

"I don't know if I'd have used the term 'bear.'" She wiped the cream from her lip with a napkin and he felt strangely disappointed.

"Whatever you want to call it, I do realize I have a temper." Jude stared at his cup, a myriad of emotions roiling his stomach. He wished he could explain himself, wished Hannah would understand. However regrettable, the truth was he *did* care what she thought of him—a lot. "I have reasons for the things I do."

Silence stretched between them, and as their gazes locked and held, Jude could see the questions in Hannah's expression. The sound of the blender made them both blink and look away.

"Why did you really ask me here today?" Hannah's manicured hands gripped her mug, the motion reminding Jude of his own tension. He made a point to relax his grip and leaned back in his chair, away from the acute level of honesty penetrating the space between them.

He looked away, trying to detach, but found himself drawn right back to Hannah's steady, chocolate-brown gaze. "I wanted to apologize. You know, for the whole bear thing."

She snorted back a laugh, and he couldn't help but grin. The seriousness of the moment won, though, and his smile drifted. "And I really do want advice about Abby. We've hit a brick wall on some topics—ones you apparently teach with ease." He spread his hands flat on the table. "How can I talk to her like you do? And even more than that, make her respond like she does to you?"

There. It was out—his vulnerability, his insecurities as a dad, all lying right there next to the studded purse she'd plopped on their table. Now if she could just give him something to go on, something new to try, he could thank her for her time and they'd have no reason to be around each other again—outside of school, anyway. They'd be separate, safe—she, far from his temper and lack of professionalism, and he, away from her explicit charm and superpower ability to weasel through his walls.

"How can you get Abby to talk to you like she does to me?" Hannah repeated. She leaned forward and touched his hand with her smaller, paler one. "That's easy. You can't."

She hated to burst Jude's bubble, but what did he expect? For Hannah to jot down some recipe for communicating with a teenager that he could follow right into a father-daughter sunset? Not happening. Besides, if he knew anything about teen girls at all, he'd realize that some topics were simply off limits to fathers.

By Jude's crestfallen expression, he obviously hadn't realized.

"It's not personal." She quickly withdrew her hand, not meaning to let it linger on his as long as it had. She rubbed her palm, already missing his warmth. "It's girl-talk. Some things resonate better from another woman, from someone who can relate."

"Someone like a mom." Jude ran both hands over the length of his face, all traces of his former confidence gone.

Despite her earlier resolve to stay removed, Hannah's heart went out to him. Temper or not, overprotective rules or not, Jude was trying his best to be a good dad. How many fathers out there would have given up long before now? Yet, because of his constant efforts, Abby had grown into a sweet, polite, intelligent girl—who now bordered on the edge of becoming a young woman. It was a difficult time even under the best of circumstances. And because of Jude's circumstances, what would normally be a trying battle could end up a full-fledged war.

"But like you said, I'm not a parent. I don't know. Maybe it will be easier than I think." It wouldn't, but she couldn't help the rash of words, hoping to ease the distress on his face. He was a good man. He shouldn't have to go through this alone. Not for the first time, Hannah pondered how unfair their situation was. Single parents were everywhere, but Abby was special. She deserved the best, not a missing link in her family. What had happened to create the void? Jude's ex might have been a model, or that might have been a rumor—but how had she died? Or why had they divorced? Obviously there was no custody agreement to share Abby, so something tragic had to occur even if it wasn't death.

She told herself she cared only for Abby's sake,

but looking into the pain in Jude's eyes, couldn't deny it was for more than just that.

Jude's hands lowered to his lap, his expression chagrined. "I shouldn't have said that about you not being a mom. It came out wrong."

"Maybe. But it's the truth." Hannah fought to keep her voice strong—and to look anywhere but at Jude's see-right-through-her blue gaze. "I shouldn't have taken it so personally." She didn't know his secrets, and he didn't know hers. Wasn't his fault she was damaged goods.

"I'm sure you're right about the woman thing." Jude let out a sigh before tipping his mug to down the last of his coffee. "In which case, I guess I'll have to hope for the best."

Judging by his expression, he knew as well as she did that wasn't much to go on. But if he refused to open up to her, tell her his reasons for the tight leash he had on Abby, there wasn't much else she could offer.

Well, maybe there was one more thing.

Hannah ran her finger around the tip of her mug. "I know I'm only around Abby a few times a week, but if she approaches me again, I promise I'll do what I can to encourage her to talk to you, too."

"That'd be nice of you." A smidgen of hope lit Jude's eyes, and Hannah felt more relief than she should have at knowing she'd help put it there. *God, what am I doing?* The automatic prayer drifted toward the wooden rafters of the coffee shop, and seemed to loiter there among the steamy haze above the barista counter. She figured her prayer didn't go farther—she hadn't spent much time talking to God since her accident, besides bemoaning how everyone else's life appeared more blessed than her own—like with her engagement couple today. Why should God listen to her now that she needed direction?

And how much did she truly care if He did?

The realization knotted her stomach, and she pushed her half-empty mug of now lukewarm coffee away from her, unable to bear another sip. She wanted to go home, away from the reminders of what she'd become, away from the pain of the truth.

Away from the man who awoke feelings in her she thought long dead.

"Can I ask you something?" Jude's husky voice tore Hannah away from her ponderings.

She quickly cleared her expression, hoping he hadn't read her own distress, and folded her hands on the table. "Shoot."

"How did you get your scar?"

She jerked, her foot kicking the table leg and sending her mug clattering across the top.

She grabbed for it the same time as Jude, their hands wrapping around the ceramic together. Heat flushed up her neck, but not in the same reaction it had when she'd touched him moments ago. No, this was the too-familiar burn of embarrassment.

"I'm sorry, I shouldn't have asked. It's none of my business." Jude dabbed the spill on the table with a pile of napkins while Hannah cleaned her mocha-splattered hands with another.

"No, it's okay." The words flew from her lips, although she didn't mean them. Would she ever stop being a freak show? Why did people care so much? She might as well make a T-shirt that simply read "Car Wreck. Don't Ask" and wear it daily.

Was that all Jude saw of her? And if he knew the rest…

The thought brought an influx of unwanted tears, and Hannah blinked rapidly to hold them back. "It's no big deal—I just realized I need to get going. It's late." She tilted her wrist to check a watch she wasn't wearing, then babbled more excuses as she gathered her purse.

Jude stood as she did, watching her with a furrowed brow—proof he didn't believe her. That was fine, she didn't believe herself. Avoiding his gaze, Hannah slung her purse strap over her arm and pushed up the sleeves of her sweater, sweat trickling down her spine. She needed air. Space. Distance.

"I really didn't mean to upset you. There I go, saying the wrong thing again." Jude's gentle touch on her forearm sent a roiling through her stomach—a total contradiction to the shame coursing through her blood. *Relax, Hannah. He doesn't know your triggers.* If her scar was only outward, didn't mirror the permanent ones on the inside, then she wouldn't react this way every time someone asked about it. For some reason, it hurt even more coming from Jude.

A reason she couldn't let herself decipher.

"Forget it, okay?" Hannah pleaded, needing him to drop it, to not make a big deal over this giant elephant in her life she couldn't control.

"If that's what you want." Jude's gaze held hers, his fingers still lightly gazing her arm.

She looked at the point of contact, then at his steady gaze, and found herself wishing she didn't mean it at all.

But like with her scars, the choice wasn't in her control.

Chapter Seven

Jude was certain the day *could* get worse, but at the moment, he wasn't entirely sure how.

He shoved away from his desk and stood facing his office window. Outside, the basketball court teemed with the sixth grade boys' gym class. He'd always made fun of the important CEOs in movies, who played virtual golf in their plush Manhattan offices or drug a mini-rake through a box of sand—but now, Jude sort of wish he had a stress reliever for himself.

He squinted at the midafternoon sunlight gleaming off the backboard on the court, unable to stop replaying in his head his date with Hannah last night. No, not date. Meeting. Thankfully—because if it had been a date, it would have gone down as the worst one in history. How could he have asked her flat out about her scar? She'd practically run away from him. Was she that sensitive about it, or did the topic simply remind her of a bad time in her life?

He truly hadn't meant to pry, but had somehow gotten caught up in the connection they'd shared about Abby, and suddenly found himself wanting to know everything about the woman his daughter trusted. In a sense, he was jealous of Hannah—she could reach his kid in a way he never had.

And at this point, probably never would.

Coach Russell Hayes, Jude's longtime friend, blew his whistle outside and gathered the group of scrawny young boys into a huddle. Head bent, he began giving what Jude knew was another one of Russell's famous pep talks. The man could coach the shyest kid into star quality. Twice now, Jude had watched a young man's career bloom on that very court under Russell. The boys had gone on to excel in high school and were offered sports scholarships for college.

Too bad Russell couldn't coach Jude out of his current predicament as easily.

As if reliving his major faux pas over and over wasn't enough to ruin his day, the email conversation between staff in Jude's inbox this morning regarding the upcoming elective decisions hadn't been positive.

"Jude, got a minute?"

Jude spun away from the window to see Head Principal Coleman in his doorway, his expression grave. "Of course."

He quickly collected himself and ushered the older man inside, indicating he should take the nicer chair behind the desk. Jude settled into the uncomfortable one where Hannah had sat not even a week ago, wishing his polite gesture to Coleman hadn't just put him out of a position of control.

And wishing his memories of Hannah didn't linger in his office like they belonged.

"I trust you got the recent string of emails?" The older man's gray mustache twitched as he pursed his lips.

"I did." Jude didn't have a real reason for not responding, other than there hadn't been anything to say—much like now. Unless he stuck his neck out, defended sports and arts, the two electives the current budget proposed axing. But really, would he be that upset to see the art department go? He hated the idea of anyone losing their jobs, but without the art department, photography lessons wouldn't uproot his plans for steering Abby in the other direction.

But if the art department went out the door, so would CREATE, and Abby loved that club. Last year, it had been the only reason she kept her grades up—in order to stay in, students had to keep a respectable grade point average. That motivation had gotten Abby through a particularly low point in her life, which was the only reason Jude hadn't yet forbidden it.

Jude cleared his throat. "Sir, if I may…"

Coleman adjusted his tie around his too-tight collar. "Speak your thoughts, son. That's why I'm here. I wanted your thoughts before the teachers' meeting. There's no going back then."

"Is the board absolutely positive there isn't another place to cut back?" Jude leaned forward, hoping to draw the older man in. "I'm picturing the outrage from parents and the community over this type of decision, and it doesn't bode well." To put it mildly. The media would be all over it, and soon their school—and Pecan Grove itself—would be harshly judged.

Coleman shifted, the chair squeaking under his weight. "I agree, but unfortunately, there doesn't seem to be any other options." He drummed his thick fingers on the desktop. "However, since your interests are invested, I'd hoped you'd put together a proposal to present to the board."

"What kind of proposal?" Jude frowned. "I've been over the budget myself. What is left to propose, if there are no other options?"

"Which elective is cut."

Jude swallowed. Oh, no. No way. "Sir, I can't possibly—"

"Both elective departments are on the chopping block—arts and sports. I'd like for you help narrow down which one is best suited for trimming."

Trimming. Ha. Jude shook his head. "You mean eliminating."

"Same difference." Coleman shrugged. "If we

had a music department it'd be up for debate, too, but we never implemented one of those. Seems former Principal Matthews realized we didn't have the money for that, either."

Thank goodness, though maybe having a third option would make choosing between the first two less impossible. Jude bit back a groan. Forget having a bad day—now it'd completely crashed and burned. How could he even be asked to make that kind of decision?

But someone had to step up, and make the best choice for the school as a whole—and obviously Coleman didn't want to do that himself. Understandably—who would? Jude squared his shoulders, determined to rise to the challenge. If the art department had to go, so be it. There'd be a whole lot less uproar over that than if the sports teams were cut. Feelings would be hurt and jobs would be lost either way, but at least if the art department went, Abby would be free of some of the influences he feared.

His thoughts flickered to Russell and the young boys on the court. Besides, who ever heard of a kid getting an art scholarship out of high school? Still…he couldn't help but picture the devastation on his daughter's face if CREATE wasn't around for her eighth grade year.

Jude briefly closed his eyes, wishing he could pray for guidance and be certain he'd actually get it. But if God would allow his wife to leave him and then die before she could see the light and raise her daughter, disrupting their family, how could He possibly care about a small decision such as this? No, as always, Jude was on his own. He'd figure it out.

Somehow.

"And Jude...."

Jude looked up as Coleman rocked forward in his chair, resting his forearms on Jude's desk. "Yes?"

"I'll need you ready to present that proposal to the board in two weeks."

Hannah joined Sophia in the extracurricular room designated for after-school clubs. "So let me get this straight." She huffed with exertion as she set her ever-present camera bag on top of a card table, one of two that had been shoved together and crowded with folding chairs. "The kids in CREATE actually *want* to learn about photography, right?"

Sophia shoved back a lock of her curly red hair as she began pulling supplies from a tote bag. "Yes. These are the ones that make my job worth it." She winked at Hannah and spread a half dozen file folders around the table, one in front of each seat. "You'll see."

Abby was the first of the students to hurry inside the classroom and take her seat—the one closest to Hannah. "Hey, Ms. Hart." She grinned at Hannah, leaning forward on her elbows. All traces of the quiet Abby from class earlier in the afternoon was gone. "Did you have fun getting coffee last night?"

Fun? Not exactly. But she couldn't say that to Jude's daughter. Hannah struggled for an honest answer as she spread some sample photos from her portfolio on the table. "The coffee was very good." Not so much the conversation, but Abby didn't have to know that.

But judging by the twinkle in Abby's eyes as she peered up at Hannah, it wasn't the coffee she was worried about.

Thankfully the rest of the club began filing inside, laughing and dumping their backpacks on the floor as they took their seats, saving Hannah from carrying the conversation further. She turned her attention to Sophia as her friend started the meeting and began going over what they would be discussing.

"I know most of you are in my art class, but not all of you." Sophia held up Hannah's sample photos. "Ms. Hart talked about lighting the other week. In case you missed it last time, she's going to do a quick review, and then I thought this smaller group would give us the chance to go over that element of photography in more detail. Ms. Hart brought some samples to show you, and…" Sophia's paused to waggle her eyebrows at the kids. "There will be homework assignments."

The small group of students, all girls except one

boy, cheered. Hannah worked to keep the shock off her face. Cheers—for homework? Wow. Sophia had a good thing going here—these were the faces of young people eager to learn and excited about art. It sort of reminded Hannah of how she felt as a young adult, the first time she realized she could actually pursue something she loved and make money at it.

And she was getting to take part in giving a bit of that back.

Hannah rose to take her place at the head of the table, noticing Abby's eyes on her with every step. It was nice to feel chosen, to be able to reach out and connect despite everything Hannah had struggled with over recent years, but she hoped it didn't stem simply from ideas Abby had about Hannah and Jude.

If it did, well, the younger girl would be sorely disappointed. Hannah had made sure of that after practically running out of the coffee shop yesterday like a child. Even now, the twinge of embarrassment from her overreaction cloaked her shoulders like a heavy, itchy wool blanket. She should have stayed, should have put on the facade she donned when put in that position, and grinned her way through it. But the concern in Jude's eyes, the interest—not curiosity, but compassion—radiating through his expression, had unnerved her. Coupled with the attraction she felt sure he saw in her eyes, well, the whole thing had been far too much for her fragile emotions to mask.

Too late to do anything about it now.

She cleared her throat and tried to focus on what really mattered—the students in front her who wanted to learn.

"Thanks for letting me crash your club, guys." Hannah smiled at the kids, and they actually smiled back. This group really was different than the general art class. "It's always fun for me to teach about what I love most." She began her presentation, using her camera to show the different light settings, and talked about the detailed features of each.

Abby was in the middle of asking a question when she interrupted herself. "Dad! What are you doing here?"

Hannah's gaze jerked to the door, where Jude had inched inside and leaned against the frame, arms crossed over his black suit. How long had he been watching her teach? She looked at Sophia, who merely shrugged.

"I'm sorry to interrupt your...club." Jude's jaw clenched as he drew nearer, taking in the material surrounding the students. Sample photos, disposable cameras, file folders full of various definitions of the parts of a camera.

Hannah felt the absurd need to step in front of the supplies and block them from his view. But that was crazy. Surely Jude didn't dislike cameras as much as he disliked his daughter being photographed.

"I need to speak with Ms. Davis. May I have a moment?" He spoke to Sophia, but his eyes darted to include Hannah. She averted her gaze, wondering if he judged her for leaving so abruptly yesterday. He wasn't the only one with secrets, nor was he the only one seemingly unwilling to share them. Still, she couldn't help but feel that if maybe he gave her an inch, she could meet him halfway.

Ridiculous. You don't owe this man a thing, Hannah, and he owes you even less.

Sophia nodded at Jude. "Of course. Guys, why you don't use your disposable cameras and take some practice shots of each other? Focus on what Ms. Hart said about lighting." Sophia gestured to the florescent lights above them. "Get creative, but take it seriously. We'll be using your photos next week at our meeting—best pictures win a prize."

Sophia motioned for Hannah to join her as she followed Jude across the room. She started to refuse, but Sophia widened her eyes in silent insistence. Hannah reluctantly joined them in the hallway, where they left the door open a crack to keep an ear on the students.

Jude started as he looked up and saw Hannah with them, but cleared his throat and played off his surprise well. "Sophia, I wanted to give you a heads-up. I know there have been rumors around school about the status of next year's budget, and well—some of them are true." He sighed, eyes weary. "The elective departments are in danger."

Sophia's brow wrinkled, and she crossed her arms over her floral-print tunic in defense. "You mean, the art department."

Jude motioned toward the closed door. "And subsequently, CREATE."

Sophia opened her mouth, but Jude held up both hands. "Nothing is official yet. But I didn't want you to get caught off guard. Since your department is one of the ones in jeopardy, I thought it only fair to warn you before the public announcement is made at the emergency teachers' meeting tomorrow."

"But that's not fair." The words blurted from Hannah's lips before she realized how immature they sounded. "I mean, I understand a budget is a budget, but surely there's something you can do. For some of these kids, art is the only part of school they enjoy. How can that be stripped away from them?" It couldn't. She'd seen the transformation herself. Maybe some of the kids took art because it was easier than a sport, but most of them enjoyed it—and the kids in CREATE downright thrived on it. Not to mention if the art department was eliminated, it would take Sophia's job with it.

Indignation stirred in Hannah's stomach, and she opened her mouth to argue further.

Jude spread his hands, cutting her off. "I understand your protests. But art is an elective—a luxury, of sorts. Not a requirement for education." He shrugged. "That's how the board sees it, anyway."

"So are sports." Sophia lifted her chin, and Hannah's stomach sank as Jude seemed to recognize the obvious challenge at the same time.

His voice clipped, he mirrored her tight stance. "I'm aware of that, Ms. Davis. And I'm taking it under consideration." Jude's tone held an unmistakable warning, his formal words indicating his restrained frustration.

She'd offended him. Likely, they both had. Hannah laid her hand on Sophia's arm, silently begging her friend not to make it worse. No man enjoyed having his authority questioned, especially a man like Jude. Sophia would only make it worse if she kept up the negativity—even if the desperation inside Hannah wanted to grab a picket sign and join her.

Sophia wilted under Hannah's touch. "I'm sorry, I'm not trying to be rude. This really caught me off guard."

"That's why I wanted you to know as soon as possible, rather than be blindsided at the meeting." Jude's gaze softened, and he cleared his throat.

"Trust me, this isn't fun for any of us. I'll be in touch if I have any more information. But Sophia…"

Both women looked up as Jude's words drifted off.

"It doesn't look good."

Chapter Eight

"This is a nightmare." Sophia stared glumly toward the twilight sky as shadows crept over Hannah's backyard, adding to the gloominess that had stuck around all afternoon since Jude's grave announcement.

Hannah pushed one foot against the floor of the patio to set the double-rocker back in motion. "Tell me about it." She passed Sophia the spray bottle of whipped cream.

Her friend tipped her head back and filled her mouth with the sweet white foam. "Too bad all of life's problems can't be solved with obscene amounts of sugar."

Hannah feigned an expression of horror. "They can't?"

"Funny." Sophia nudged her in the side.

Hannah rocked them again. "Seriously, Sophia, if you get laid off, you know you can crash here."

"I know." Sophia exhaled loudly, leaning her

head back to rest against the wooden rocker. "You say laid off, but it feels like fired."

Hannah took the whipped cream back and snapped the lid over the dispenser. "It's not personal, though. It's business."

"What are you talking about? It's art. It's incredibly personal." Sophia turned her head, meeting Hannah's gaze. "Do you not consider your photographs personal? Do you not put a little of yourself into every one? I've put myself into my career, into my students. Into their dreams. It's incredibly personal."

Ouch. Sophia was right. Hannah could only relate too well—it *was* a little personal, regardless of what the school thought or said. "Being laid off won't change who you are, though."

"No, but I'll lose the opportunity to make a difference for those kids in the only way I know how."

Also true. Hannah lifted her face to the stars beginning to poke through the evening sky. It wasn't only her friend's job on the line, but her very essence. Sophia could get a job teaching elsewhere, but to have to leave Pecan Grove and all her family and friends? That wasn't the answer. And who would pick up the slack with the kids at the school? The students who needed Sophia's vibrancy and compassion, her inspiration and creativity?

"You told Jude yourself, these kids don't deserve this." The wind lifted Sophia's hair, teasing tendrils across her face, and she didn't bother to swipe them back. "A lot of them will suffer if the art department is cut out. For some of the kids, it's the only thing they're good at, the only part of school that gives them a feeling of accomplishment and worth." She sighed. "I wish I could afford to at least keep CREATE going on my own. But I don't think I can—especially not if I get fired." She snorted.

"Laid off."

"Whatever."

Hannah nibbled on her lower lip. "So what can we do?" She hated this feeling of helplessness, of injustice. She'd told Jude it wasn't fair—but it also wasn't his fault. She didn't know much about the inner workings of the public school system, but she could bet the decision wasn't Jude's alone, but rather the entire school board, along with the opinion and influence of the head principal. Jude was likely in the position of messenger earlier this afternoon, which had to be uncomfortable. No wonder he'd been so torn between formal and empathetic. He needed to be in control, but probably hated the turn of events as much as Sophia did.

"Wait and see, I guess." Sophia scooted down on the swing and folded her hands across her stomach. "What else is there?"

"That seems so passive."

"I'm an art teacher, not the cheerleading coach."

"But why can't we hold some fundraisers?"

Sophia shot her a look. "I think if the budget

crisis could be solved with a bake sale and a car wash, the school board would have suggested that already."

"Any effort would be better than none. We need to at least raise awareness, if nothing else. Get the kids involved—especially CREATE." Hannah sat forward, twisting in the rocker to face her friend. "It's their club—they should be able to have a say in this. Besides, the only thing worse than going down with a fight is not putting up one at all, right?"

"So, you want to have a bake sale? Hannah, I can't cook, and I bet most of those kids in CREATE can't, either." She wrinkled her nose. "Not to be rude, but I still remember those brownies you tried to—"

"Not a bake sale." Hannah flitted one hand in the air. "Something bigger, more artistic. Something the kids already excel at." A dozen ideas swam through Hannah's mind, replacing her earlier dismay with a flush of enthusiasm. "Let's ask them at the next CREATE meeting. At any rate, we could have a series of fundraisers. Spread them out throughout the year, so we can bringing in money as the semester passes." She took a breath as her ideas continued to churn. "Maybe even pitch the idea to Jude, and try to get the board behind us. Who knows what could happen!"

Sophia still looked skeptical as she took the

can of whipped cream from Hannah's hands and sprayed another mouthful.

Hannah frowned. "Look, do you want a job next fall, or not?"

"When you put it that way…" Sophia snorted. "I just don't want to get the kids' hopes up and it not work out. They're going to be disappointed enough with the announcement tomorrow. What if they try something big and fail?"

"Isn't that life? Trying, failing, trying again, and then succeeding?" Hannah's confidence grew as the idea warmed. "If any of them decide to seriously pursue photography as a career one day, or any artistic venture for that matter, they have to learn to take risks." She shrugged. "If it doesn't work, then consider this one last life lesson you taught them."

"Maybe you should have been a defense lawyer instead of a photographer." Sophia grinned as she handed over the whipped cream. "Okay, I'm in. We'll brainstorm ideas Friday at the next CREATE meeting."

"This will be good. I can feel it." Hannah shook the spray can. "Since we have a plan now, I think it's safe to say this calls for ice cream and chocolate sauce."

"That's definitely less desperate-looking." Sophia followed Hannah into the condo's cherry-print kitchen. "Speaking of looking desperate— you never did tell me how your coffee date with

Jude went last night." Her eyes sparkled with mischief. "I think he was pretty desperate to see you outside of school."

Hannah opened the freezer and took out a gallon of ice cream, her previously lifted mood suddenly soured. "He wasn't, believe me. And it wasn't a date. I told you that."

"And you still believe it?" Sophia snagged two red bowls from the cabinet.

"Trust me. Jude would never be interested in me that way."

Sophia raised one eyebrow. "And you, him?"

"Doesn't matter. We're not right for each other." Hannah stabbed the ice cream with the scooper a little harder than she meant to. "He's used to models, and I'm, well, obviously not one." Her face burned as she plopped another scoop of ice cream into the bowl Sophia held out. Talk about the understatement of the year. Unless maybe she modeled for a scar cream commercial—as the *before* picture.

Sophia's eyes narrowed. "Hannah, it's a scar. You're not a monster. You're beautiful."

"And you're my best friend, so I appreciate the obligatory compliments."

"They're not oblig— Hannah, come on." Sophia set the bowl on the counter and planted her hands on her hips. "All right. You gave me a pep talk, now it's your turn."

"No, seriously, I'm fine. Facts are facts." Hannah

kept her attention on the scooper in her hand. "Besides, even if I thought of him that way, there's Abby's best interest to consider. And Jude is like my temporary boss. There's too many odd factors involved here."

"All of which sound pretty temporary."

Hannah finally met Sophia's gaze. "Yeah—unless Jude ends up firing my best friend."

Sophia bit her lip. "You said laid off earlier. I liked that better."

"Hopefully it won't matter soon. We have a plan, remember?" Hannah tried to force her thoughts off Jude and offered a feeble smile. "It'll work out and everyone will get what they want. You'll keep your job, Jude and the school board will keep their budget in check and the kids will keep their club. Win-win." She squinted. "Win."

"And what about you? What do you get?"

Hannah grabbed two spoons from the drawer and handed one to Sophia. "This isn't about me."

Sophia's gaze lingered. "Then maybe it's about time something is."

"No. I've been focused on myself for too long as it is." Hannah caught a glimpse of her reflection in the darkness of the kitchen window above the sink, and pointedly looked away. "I need distractions. I need to give back."

What she really needed was to rid her entire house of mirrors. But that would be giving in. She wouldn't cave that completely. She'd come this far.

Her stomach twinged, and she emphatically shoved her spoon into her bowl.

Now if only she could start seeing her scar for what it was, and not what it represented.

The following Friday, Sophia insisted they hold their CREATE meeting outside on the school lawn, under the row of oak trees in front of the school.

"Maybe the fresh air will help us think." Hannah helped Sophia spread a thick blanket on the ground picnic-style over the grass sprinkled with autumn leaves. The students dumped their backpacks at the base of one of the trees and began rummaging for their notebooks.

Sophia smoothed the blanket flat before sitting down and draping her long skirt over her ankles. "We'll need all the help we can get, that's for sure."

Hannah started to say that maybe they should pray, but the words tasted hypocritical on her tongue. She clamped her lips together as she cast a glance at the pristine blue sky, free of clouds this sunny afternoon. She hadn't even prayed about this ordeal yet privately—she could hardly expect Sophia to jump on board with the concept, especially since her friend had never shown much interest in faith. Besides, did Hannah really even believe God would answer after she'd all but turned her back on Him after the accident? Still, He had to care about the welfare of the kids and Sophia's job—right?

She didn't know what she believed anymore. Her car windows hadn't been the only thing that shattered that fateful afternoon.

The younger girls quickly joined Hannah and Sophia on the blanket, Abby claiming the spot closet to Hannah. Peter, the only boy in the group, chose to sit on the grass—a good two feet away from any of the females. Sophia teasingly rolled her eyes at him before calling the meeting to official order. "Who did their homework?"

Everyone in the group raised their hands. Lana, a pretty brunette with glasses, waved her arm enthusiastically. "Can I share mine first?"

"Sure." Sophia pulled a spiral notebook from her bag and opened it to a clean page. "But before we dive into that, Ms. Hart and I have something we need to discuss with all of you."

The official announcement about the budget cuts had been announced at a teachers' meeting Thursday, as Jude had forewarned. Sophia told Hannah last night the response from the group was pretty much what she'd guessed—outrage and panic from staff and parents alike.

Hannah took in the smiling, eager young faces on the blanket around her, and hoped her idea to fight the budget wouldn't turn out to be a bad one. These kids deserved every chance they had to keep the club they loved.

But would their one chance be enough?

"Some of you might have heard what happened

at the teachers' meeting yesterday." Sophia twirled her pencil between her fingers. "But if you didn't, basically, the art department is in danger. Electives are being cut from next year's budget, and if the art department goes, so does CREATE."

"What?"

"Why?"

A few of the girls mumbled various shocked exclamations, while Lana's face grew pale. Peter remained silent, but his dark brows furrowed over his eyes into a deep frown.

Sophia held up both hands for attention. "I know, it stinks. And trust me, if I had the money to keep this club running without the support from the art department, I would. But without the stipend we get from the department budget, we wouldn't be able to do all the things we're used to. Not even close."

One of the girls, Mya, shot a hard look at Abby. "Can't your dad do something?"

Abby shrugged, but two patches of pink immediately flushed her cheeks. "I doubt it. He doesn't run the school."

"Yes, he does," Lana argued. "Just tell him you don't want him to do this."

"Guys, guys." Sophia clapped, interrupting the building tension. "It's not that easy. This isn't Abby's fault—or Principal Bradley's."

Hannah jumped in. "Instead of pointing fingers, let's focus on finding ways to raise money so nothing gets cut." She gestured to the empty notebook in Sophia's lap. "We need a list of ideas to get started. Who can think of one?"

The students stared blankly at Hannah, and she tried not to imagine their gazes flickering over her scar. Ducking her head a little, she swung her hair over her cheek. "Come on, gang. Think." *And quit staring at me.*

Peter finally looked up from where he was splitting a blade of grass in two. "I can think of ways to earn enough money for, like, an MP3 player—but not an entire department at a school. Isn't that thousands of dollars?"

"Yes. But it's okay to start small. There's nothing wrong with that." Hannah smiled with encouragement, glad everyone's gaze was now redirected to Peter. "What are you thinking?"

He shifted in the grass. "Well, you know, maybe a car wash. Or a lemonade stand. My twin sisters did that last summer and made seventy-five dollars in a single weekend."

"My mom had a garage sale last month and made over one hundred dollars," Lana suggested. Her lip poked out in a pout. "But she didn't give me any of it."

"Those are all good ideas." Sophia scribbled in her notebook. "But we'd have to do them all—several times each—to make any significant money for the school. It would help, but it won't come close to being enough to cover the entire budget allowance for the department. We need to think bigger if we want to even make a dent."

Abby, who'd been quiet ever since Mya and Lana accused her dad, nibbled on the edge of her pinky nail. "What if we make a magazine?"

The group fell so silent, Hannah could hear the tree frogs chirping in the branches above them. "What kind of magazine, Abby?" She prompted.

"One we could sell to raise money. We could write the articles in it, and list all the upcoming fundraisers we plan for the rest of the year, so everyone knows when they are. That would raise awareness, right?" She picked at a thread on her plain jeans, so different than the other girls' rhinestone-studded pairs, looking up at Hannah's encouraging nod. "We could take the pictures, too."

"That's a great idea." Hannah's brain jumped into turbo-mode, her previous insecurities about her scar shoved to the background as she matched Abby's enthusiasm. "I could do the photo development at my studio for free."

"And we could do the magazine layout with the yearbook committee's computer programs." Sophia nodded, eyes sparkling with hope for the first time since Jude's impromptu visit to her classroom.

"I'll ask Mr. Jenkins." Lana slipped her hand in the air. "I'm on the yearbook committee."

"That'd be very helpful, Lana." Sophia made a few more notations in her notebook. "If we all work together, I think this could really make a difference."

"Yeah, it sounds like this won't cost much at all to produce. We could sell the magazine, and between those profits and the ones from the actual fundraisers throughout the year, we could actually make some money." Hannah reached over and tweaked Abby's hair. "Smart thinking, girl."

Abby grinned, her earlier blush now hidden under the glow of praise. Hannah's heart warmed toward her another degree. Did Jude have any idea how talented and sweet his daughter was? Or was he was so caught up in the outer details that he didn't realize what lay buried beneath the surface?

"Even if we don't raise enough money with the magazine and the fundraisers, we're at least raising awareness." Sophia nodded. "I like it. We might as well." She began doling out assignments, which the students carefully wrote in their own folders. "And guess what? As a bonus—why don't you guys not only take the pictures, but model, too? We could even do a fashion layout!"

Peter groaned, but a chorus of cheers rose from the girls, Abby's the loudest of them all. Hannah's gaze drifted somewhere toward her boot-clad feet.

She could only imagine what Jude would have to say about that.

Chapter Nine

"You shoot like a girl." Russell Hayes caught the basketball that bounced off the backboard and threw it to Jude.

Fanning the neck of his saturated T-shirt, Jude narrowed his eyes. "I'm the principal, not the basketball coach."

Russell grinned, having barely even worked up a sweat despite the half hour they'd already spent on the inside court—and despite the thirty pounds he had on Jude.

Jude drew a deep breath and tried to focus on the rim, but his second attempt rebounded just as wildly as his first. Talk about his head not being in the game. He thought coming down to the school gym Friday night to shoot baskets with his friend would relieve stress, not add to it. Not that Russell cared how well Jude played, but his sorry game felt like one more thing in his life going wrong.

Russell made an easy layup, then hooked the

ball under his arm and faced Jude, who reached up and wiped his forehead with his shirt. "What gives, man? I always beat you, but not this bad." He winked. "Maybe we should have played C-O-N-S-T-A-N-T-I-N-O-P-L-E instead of H-O-R-S-E. Give you a fighting chance."

Jude snorted back a laugh. "I doubt it'd have mattered."

"So what's up?" Russell's teasing expression faded as understanding dawned. "Is it the school budget?"

Jude held out his hands for the ball, which Russell tossed to him. "There's no way to win. Regardless of which elective goes, people will get hurt, parents will get upset, kids will be affected." And so on. The cycle would continue down the chain until there was a mess of destruction for him to clean up. People, especially in a small town, didn't let this kind of thing go easily, especially when their kids were involved. Whichever decision Jude made, he'd be hearing about it well into the next year.

Russell rubbed one hand over his nearly shaved head, looking as lost as Jude felt. "I'm sure it's not easy."

"That's the understatement of the year." Jude took careful aim, released, and the ball swished against the net—the bottom side. Good grief. Maybe if he could land a basket, he could quit caring so much about a sport he actually had no interest in, outside of it being his friend's profession.

The profession that might not last very much longer.

Jude's stomach knotted as Russell jogged to retrieve the ball. "What would you do if the sports department was eliminated?" What kind of friend would Jude be if he was responsible for letting Russell's coach position slip through the cracks? Then again, what kind of man would he be to intentionally let anyone's job go—including Sophia's?

Russell lined up for a three-pointer, his shoes squeaking on the shiny floor. "Keep teaching math, I suppose, and wait it out. The money might cycle back around."

"And if it doesn't?" It wouldn't, by the looks of things. Jude hated to use the word *permanent,* but with today's economy, he couldn't imagine the budget finding room to reinstate an eliminated department anytime soon—if ever. Certainly not to the level it used to be.

Russell shrugged as his next shot dropped cleanly through the basket. "It'd be rough. But I guess I'll cross that bridge then, you know? One door closes, another opens, and all that."

"That's a lot of clichés for a basketball court."

Russell laughed, the sound reverberating along the gym's walls. "Okay, fine. You want a sports analogy? Then I'll keep playing offensive until I need to switch to defensive. Or, I'll keep my head in the game and my body on the field until they call a time-out."

"Those were worse." Jude took the ball from Russell and twirled it on one finger, the only sports trick he had in his arsenal. He used to entertain Abby with that for hours when she was little—especially in the months after Miranda's death, when Jude had grown desperate to hear Abby's giggles, desperate for normal. Her pudgy fingers would try to hold the ball upright, and every time it would fall, she'd laugh hysterically. Somehow, she never got frustrated that she couldn't do it. She'd just try again—or hand Jude the ball to watch his trick again.

Jude wished he could shake off his own failures as easily. But they clung to him like the sweaty shirt on his back, sticking to the fabric of his soul and refusing to budge.

"I always wished I could do that." Russell gestured to the ball still rotating on the tip of Jude's finger.

"Yeah, well, I wish I could make any shot I attempted." Jude stopped the ball mid-twirl and bounced it to Russell. "And I wish this budget crisis would go away. Did I tell you Coleman placed the entire thing on my shoulders?"

"I'm not surprised." Russell dribbled the ball twice before catching it and holding it against his side. "What are you going to do?"

"That, my friend, is the million-dollar question."

And at the moment, he hadn't a clue. "Technically the decision isn't mine. I'm only preparing the proposal for the board." He hesitated. "Though according to Coleman, whatever I present will likely be chosen."

Russell frowned. "I didn't mean, what choice will you make. I meant, how will you go about making it?"

Jude wiped a ribbon of sweat from his eyebrows. "Same way I do everything else. Detailed planning, organization, charts and graphs to back up the—" He cut himself off at Russell's incessant headshake. "What?"

"Wrong formula."

Now the math analogies were coming out, but Jude bit back the remark at the serious sheen in Russell's eyes. "How so?"

"You're missing a key factor." Russell threw Jude the ball. "Prayer."

Jude swallowed the bitter retort rising in his throat, focusing instead on the ball in his hands. He ran his thumb over the rubbery, bumpy surface. "That hasn't worked so well for me."

"Come on, you can't play the game without a coach." Russell pointed to the gym ceiling.

Jude's gaze followed, narrowing against the brightness of the florescent lights. He let out a long breath. "He benched me a long time ago."

Russell scoffed. "Not true. You benched yourself."

Jude winced, but the words rang solid. Maybe it

was more his fault than God's, though lately the details felt pretty mixed up. The only thing he knew for sure was at one point in his life, he had a solid connection to the Lord. Now the connection had lost power, and Jude floundered. Badly. Maybe he faked making do on his own for a while, but with Abby's teenage years barreling toward him like an out-of-control freighter, it wouldn't hurt to have some backup again. Someone to call out the plays for him, as Russell would say.

"Maybe you're right." Jude dribbled the ball, then shot from the three-point line. It circled the rim once before dropping off to the side. "But I still don't think God cares as much as you say He does. Not about the details."

"Why do you think that?" Russell retrieved the ball, but didn't throw it back.

"He took Abby's mom from her. From me." Jude pinched the bridge of his nose with his fingers, avoiding eye contact with his friend who had always been able to see a little more than Jude wanted. "And if you say He didn't, than the only other explanation is that I drove her off." He licked his dry lips. "Neither option feels good."

"You've got to quit carrying that around, man. It's over—done. You know Miranda made her own choices." Russell pointed his finger at him, a move Jude had seem him make a hundred times to his ball players. "You have enough stress for today, so stop packing the past in your backpack, too." He punctuated his next statement with air jabs. "The only thing you need to carry is faith."

"If it were that easy, I'd have dropped the backpack long ago." Jude tugged his shirt over the waist of his athletic shorts. "Is that how you don't even seem to care that you could lose a significant portion of your income in a few months? Faith?"

Russell frowned. "You make it sound trivial."

Wasn't it? What did having faith really change? Bad things would happen regardless—Jude was living proof of that. But he couldn't force the words past his lips. So he shrugged.

"Come to church with me Sunday. It's been years."

Jude shook his head before his friend even finished speaking. "No thanks. Not yet." Maybe not ever. He couldn't be disappointed again. If God hadn't been there when he needed Him most, why should Jude make another effort? He was tired of being let down—by people, and by the Divine.

"If not for you, then do it for Abby."

That stopped him. Jude tilted his head to one side and planted his hands on his waist. "Now you're cheating."

Russell threw the ball at him, a little harder than before. "It's called strategy." He smiled. "And it's for your own good."

Abby hadn't been to church since Jude's parents took her in the years after Miranda left. At the time, Jude played off his own lack of attendance, blaming it on needing to work and make a way for his daughter. Eventually his parents stopped nit-picking, and soon Abby preferred sleeping in over learning Bible stories.

Jude slowly dribbled the ball as he debated. Maybe Abby's attitude of late would be different if she started attending church regularly again. It certainly couldn't hurt. There were several teachers at the school who went to church on a steady basis, and he couldn't help but notice how their personalities differed from other teachers in regards to patience and morals.

No wonder Russell thought Jude needed to go back himself.

His thoughts flitted to Hannah, and to the goodness she radiated despite her obvious insecurities over her scar. Was she a Christian? The way she opened up to Abby, took her under her proverbial wing and drew her out, seemed like something a Christian would do. Maybe Abby could absorb some of those positive qualities by being in church again.

Problem was, Jude couldn't make Abby go without going himself.

He weighed the pros and cons, then lined up his next shot, futile as it might be after all his previous misses. "Fine. Sunday it is."

The ball swished neatly through the net.

Editing photos on a Friday night.

Hannah took a swig of her diet soda. At one

point long ago, the reality of her weekend choices would have embarrassed her, but tonight, it felt a lot like what the rest of her life had come to—resignation.

She touched up the glare from the client's glasses in the picture before her, debating putting the project aside completely until she could focus better. But she told the customer she'd have their disk of edited pictures ready by Monday, so there wasn't much time left. She just needed to clear her head and focus.

Which was a little hard to do when every click of her mouse reminded her of editing Abby's photo. Who would have thought a single click of the camera shutter at the park could have started such an awful chain of events?

But was every part of it awful? Her conscience taunted her. No, not all of it. Upsetting Jude by giving him the photo was definitely not a highlight of her time at Pecan Grove Junior High, and neither was creating conflict between him and Abby. But sitting across from Jude at the coffee shop, catching a glimpse of his vulnerability and rare level of love for his daughter seemed to outweigh the negative. Not to mention the moments she felt—however inaccurately—that she might actually have a chance of catching his eye.

She couldn't deny the attraction she felt for Jude Bradley any longer, despite his temper, despite his quirks. Her feelings went deeper than simply admiring his physical qualities—though there were certainly those.

Hannah tapped her finger absently on her computer mouse. Something indefinable in Jude resonated with something inside herself. Regret? Loss? She couldn't quite name it, and a piece of heart continually warned her that was for the best. What would pining after a man like Jude do for her, other than drag her self-esteem even further through the mud?

Oops. Great, now she'd given her client a purple eye, instead of removing the red. Hannah undid her mistake, then saved the program and closed the screen window. So much for working tonight. Maybe she should call it quits and curl up in bed with a book.

Not that that wasn't any less pathetic than working on the weekend. Sophia was single, but she probably wasn't sitting around grading papers. Her best friend dated—casually, maybe, but at least she got out on the town regularly and enjoyed someone's company.

Instead of hiding her face from the world—literally.

Hannah's cell phone rang on the desk beside her. She swiped it up as she stood and carried her nearly empty can to the kitchen. "Hello?"

"Hannah, it's Jude."

She tripped on the carpet, dropping the aluminum can as she caught herself against the kitchen counter. Soda splattered across the floor and she stared at it blindly. Her heart stammered a beat, traitorous to the alarms blaring a warning not to overact—too late. Was Jude sitting at home on a Friday night, too? Thinking of her? Her cheeks warmed with hope. No, not hope. Hadn't she just talked herself out of that? *Snap out of it, Hannah.*

Jude paused. "Is this a bad time? Sophia gave me your number, said you'd be at home."

Hannah cleared her throat to compose herself, while envisioning kicking her best friend in the rear. So much for impressions. "No, it's fine. I was just finishing up some work." She winced as she tossed the can into the recycle bin. Now he knew she might as well be the proverbial old maid. All she needed were sixteen cats to complete the picture.

She had to remember to quit caring what he thought.

"Ah, working on Friday night. I've certainly been there before." Jude's voice seemed deeper over the phone, and Hannah tried to ignore the quiver in her stomach at the husky sound. "I'm sorry to interrupt, but I had a question." He chuckled, though it sounded more tense than natural. "An odd question."

"Sure. Go ahead." Hannah grabbed a paper towel and squatted to clean up the mess, trying to steady the childish pounding of her pulse. He probably wanted to know something else about Abby, another girl-trick that wouldn't work unless he somehow morphed into a mother overnight.

"Do you go to church?"

Shock pummeled Hannah in the gut and she rocked back on her heels. He might as well have asked her if she played poker at the pool hall. "Do I *what?*"

Jude hesitated. "Is that a no?"

"Yes. I mean, no, it isn't a no." The silence stretched as Hannah pressed her fingers against her pounding temples. What *did* she mean? "I used to go regularly, but haven't…lately." That is, if two years counted as lately. But why did Jude care? Maybe this was another weird date-that-wasn't-a-date attempt—first coffee, now church. What game was the man playing?

"I told you it was an odd question." Jude's laugh sounded a little more genuine this time. "The whole thing is somewhat odd for me, too. A friend of mine invited me to attend his church this Sunday, and well—like you, I haven't been lately."

The true confessions thing was endearing, but again, why was she involved in this sudden self-evaluation? Had she somehow become his unofficial life coach during the course of their interactions at school? Just because she knew how to talk to teenagers on their level didn't mean Jude needed her input on his life, too—in fact, he'd made it quite clear that he didn't. Hannah stood and tossed the soda-saturated napkin into the trash. "Then I think you should go."

She headed to the chair in her living room. Apparently this conversation would take a while. Though she wasn't exactly complaining—talking to a handsome professional on a Friday night sounded a whole lot less cat-lady than working.

"I intend to." Jude cleared his throat, a touch of nerves coating his voice once again. "I called because I hoped you'd come, too."

It was a good thing she had sat back down. Hannah dug her fingers into the soft upholstery of the chair as her hopes flared. "Me?"

"It was Abby's idea. I asked if she would go with me Sunday, and she said she would—but only if you did, too."

He let out a long exhale, giving Hannah time to wrap her mind around her disappointment. *Abby* wanted her to come. Not Jude.

"What do you think?"

She thought it'd be a whole lot easier to *stop* thinking about Jude, if he quit asking her what she thought all the time. But she couldn't exactly tell him that. She closed her eyes, wishing her call waiting would beep, or a deliveryman would knock on her door, or Sophia would drop by with donuts—anything to give her a legitimate excuse to avoid his question. To hide. To go back to her cave of a workroom and edit until she could picture something other than his electric-blue gaze staring at her over coffee.

"Hello? Are you there?"

Hannah forced out a quick response. "Yes, sorry. Just…thinking."

"So you'll come Sunday?" The question lifted his voice, and she could almost imagine those dark, perfectly-shaped eyebrows lifting on his forehead as he waited for her answer. For Abby. Not him.

As much as she wanted to be there for the girl, the whole thing rubbed Hannah the wrong way. Maybe because she got her hopes up that Jude wanted to see her again outside of school. But no, this was only another reminder that Jude was only interested in her in regard to the pedestal on which Abby had propped Hannah.

She wracked her brain for a viable excuse. "Sophia and I usually have brunch on Sundays." Oops. That gave away exactly what her definition of "lately" entailed. Not that Jude would judge her church attendance if his own hadn't been stellar. Regardless, eating bagels and cream cheese with her best friend sounded a whole lot more appetizing than sitting next to Jude on a padded pew, all too aware of all the reasons why he would never think of her the way she wished he would.

"Can you ladies reschedule this once?" Jude asked. "For Abby's sake. She really thinks highly of you, Hannah."

Hannah squeezed the arm of the chair, then released her grip with a soft sigh. "All right. Sunday it is. I'll try to bring Sophia with me."

"That'd be great." Jude sounded relieved—because the more the merrier? Maybe he thought if there was a crowd it wouldn't be so intimate sitting with just her and Abby. Way too cozy a scene.

Though it'd have been nice to at least get to pretend to be part of a family for a little while.

"It's Pecan Grove Community Church." Jude quickly gave her directions, which Hannah didn't write down because she already knew. She'd driven past the pristine white church and admired its beautiful stained glass windows from afar many times. Sometimes she felt she should slip inside and leave an offering in the plate simply for getting to admire the building. Now she could see those windows up close—and leave a twenty-dollar bill.

Maybe that would alleviate some of the guilt she felt for paying more attention to the external than the internal.

It felt good calling Hannah at the end of the day, when the house was quiet and the only sounds were the ticking of the wall clock and the hum of the heater kicking on. It felt natural. Right. Comforting. All the things Jude had no business feeling for her at this point in his life. Oh, who was he kidding? Maybe ever.

Still, a man could get used to hearing Hannah's soft-spoken voice every night.

Jude stretched in his recliner, the cordless phone still in his hand, warm from his tight grip. He was really looking forward to seeing her Sunday—for Abby, of course. Not for himself.

Though he was having a harder time than usual remembering all the reasons why that was true.

Slam.

Abby shut the front door harder than necessary—as usual—as headlights from her ride flashed across the windows before disappearing. Jude never could tell when the preteen was mad or simply took her youthful excitement out on the hinges.

He sat up straight as Abby bounced into the living room, relieved her smile seemed genuine tonight and not sarcastic or guarded. Maybe they'd actually get through the evening without a fight. Their conversation on the phone earlier in the evening, when he'd called to ask her about church, had gone well enough. He smiled back. "You must have had a good time at Sarah's house."

"Yep." Abby kept bouncing toward the fridge, where she took out a canned soda despite the fact it was already after 9:00 p.m. He started to protest, then stopped. It was Friday night and Jude hated to ruin her good mood because of a little late-night caffeine. He'd get her back on routine tomorrow.

She popped the top and took a long swig, her eyes still bright. From the looks of it, she'd be up awhile anyway, regardless of the extra sugar. "Lana and Mya were there, too, so we got a head start on the magazine."

"Wait. What magazine?" Jude frowned, his own good mood fading. Surely the girls weren't over there at Sarah's house, pouring over fashion magazines. Abby knew the rules. He could occasionally look past sodas and sugar, but some things weren't negotiable. There were better options for reading material than that.

"The magazine we're doing for CREATE. Duh." Abby sank down on the couch across from him, soda in hand. Then she slapped one hand dramatically against her forehead. "Oh, wait! I totally forgot to tell you. You distracted me with all that church stuff." She laughed sheepishly.

"Then by all means, fill me in." Jude didn't hide his teasing sarcasm as Abby stuck her tongue out at him.

She resumed a straight face, her good mood radiating even from her slumped position on the sofa. "At our CREATE meeting this afternoon we brainstormed ideas on how to save the art department—and our club."

Jude nodded. "That's good." If the extracurricular clubs got involved, they might actually stand a chance of raising some money for next year's elective budget. It wouldn't fix the problem, but any additional funds could maybe delay things by a semester.

But one obvious question remained.

"How exactly does a magazine play into a fundraiser?" Tension bunched in Jude's shoulders and he rotated his neck, trying to ward it off. *Don't overact,* he coached himself. *Just hear her out.* Yet the knots doubled.

"We're making a magazine to sell for profit, and advertise the rest of the fundraisers we'll plan for the year." Abby gestured so wildly with her can, Jude half expected the carbonated liquid to fly out. "We're writing the articles, and Ms. Hart is helping us take the pictures. She's even going to develop them in her studio for free! Isn't that cool of her?"

"Very cool." Jude's teeth gritted and he clamped his jaw to keep from saying more. All the warm thoughts of Hannah flew from his mind as he pictured the cute photographer leading Abby straight toward his worst nightmare. Hannah might not know Jude's story or why he felt the way he did any more than Abby, but after the debacle in his office over that photo, one would think she'd have gotten the hint of his preferences.

"And the best part is…" Abby paused dramatically as she stood and twirled in a circle. "We're all going to be the models!"

"Oh, no, you're not!" The words flew out, harder and louder than Jude anticipated. But he didn't stop to take them back. "You know the rules, Abby. No magazines. No modeling. No fancy clothes." His list silently continued, an endless rant in his mind that was too little, too late for the only other woman he'd ever loved. *No head shots. No agents. No affairs.*

No drugs.

Abby's face paled as she flopped back on the sofa. This time, her drink did spill, but she didn't notice and Jude didn't care. "Why do you have to be so mean? None of the other parents care about this stuff! You're so weird!"

Jude drew a deep breath as he stood, a rush of indignation tempting him to blurt out the truth. But that wouldn't do any good. He'd rather be the bad guy yet again, than have Abby feel abandoned or ashamed of their past. Besides, it wasn't her fault Miranda left.

It was his.

"It doesn't matter if you understand or not. Rules are rules, and you're under my authority. That's the way it is." He crossed his arms over his chest, partly to display that authority, and partly to hide the way his helpless frustration made his hands shake.

Abby jumped up, eyes sparking with indignation, and for a moment, Jude wished he could erase the past five minutes and have his daughter in front of him, happy and smiling and excited about a school project. But why did it have to be *this* project?

She set her drink on the end table and crossed her arms, mirroring his stance. She might have her mother's bone structure and sass, but her temper was all Jude's doing.

Just one more way he'd mess up his kid just like he did his marriage.

"Fine," she snapped. "Everyone in my club thinks this whole budget thing is your fault anyway. So go ahead, prove them right! Thanks a lot."

She stomped toward the stairs and Jude let her go, wishing he could call her back and have the right words to make it better. Wishing he could break down the wall she'd thrown up around her.

And mostly wishing she hadn't been right.

Chapter Ten

"I can't believe you talked me into this." Sophia paused in the foyer of the church and bent to adjust the strap on her high-heeled shoe.

Hannah grabbed Sophia's arm to keep her friend from toppling over. "I'm as uncomfortable as you, trust me." She glanced down at Sophia's shoes, then at her own worn-in leather boots. "Though my feet don't hurt. Have you ever worn heels before?"

"If you count wedges." Sophia finally stood upright and hitched her purse higher on her shoulder. "These are new." Her ankle-length skirt swirled around her knees as she kicked one leg out to show them off.

"You bought new shoes for church?" Hannah started to jest, then stopped, wondering if she should have done the same thing instead. What if everyone else looked more like Sophia? Or what if Sophia was the one overdressed, and her friend's first church experience was negatively tainted?

Not that Hannah had much business worrying about her friend's spiritual status when her own had been on life support the past twenty-four months.

She cast an anxious glance at the people entering the sanctuary, attempting to discreetly observe their outfits. Most of them smiled or nodded at her, though some seemed oblivious to the newcomers and focused on their bulletins instead. Judging by the plethora of suits, pressed slacks and silk blouses, it wouldn't have hurt to make a better impression than boots and a simple navy sweaterdress.

One older man's eyes met hers, then dropped slightly to linger on her scar. Hannah reached up and adjusted her hair, swinging it across her cheek. He abruptly looked away and kept moving, but it didn't stop an embarrassed flush from heating Hannah's neck. Would there ever be a reprieve from the stares?

"There they are!" Jude's familiar voice, tinged with relief, sounded from down the crowded hallway. Hannah looked up in time to see him and Abby threading their way through the throngs of people, like salmon swimming upstream.

"Hey, guys." Hannah smiled, but her discomfort grew at the shadows clouding Abby's eyes. The teenager's arms were crossed defensively over her flower-print dress, which looked better suited to the styling of a six-year-old. Or maybe a grandmother. "Good morning."

"Mornin'." Abby avoided eye contact, and from the wide berth she gave her dad, it wasn't a good morning at all. So much for Hannah's presence helping Abby adjust to the idea of church. The teen looked ready to charge through the doors back into the parking lot like a bull from a chute.

"We're glad you're here." Jude nudged Abby with his elbow, but she refused to look up. "Both of us."

Hannah tried to lighten the mood settling over them, forcing a chipper perk to her voice. "Thanks for inviting me. It's good to be here."

"For some of us more than others," Sophia mumbled. She clutched her purse and looked over her shoulder toward the doors, as if she too might hightail it back outside if only she could be sure to get away with it without tripping over her new shoes.

Hannah bit back a sigh. Now Sophia and Abby were both making it clear they'd rather be elsewhere. Talk about awkward. She looked back at Jude. It was growing harder by the minute not to drink in Jude's polished look. He'd worn a blue suit today with a white dress shirt and blue-and-green tie that did crazy things for his eyes—and apparently Hannah wasn't the only one who noticed. Several women of varying ages cast appreciative stares as they walked by, offering shy smiles. Did Jude have any idea the effect he had on the female population, even in church? Or was he so consumed with his job and his daughter he'd written off romance altogether? Not that Hannah was in the running. She could easily count three women in the foyer alone who were better matches for Jude. If he wanted another model, he wouldn't have to look far.

Quit it, Hannah. You're in church. Focus.

"Should we go inside?" Hannah linked her arm through her friend's, in case she was still debating escape. No use standing in the hallway any longer with exit doors tempting Sophia on all sides—and especially not with the daggers Abby kept shooting her dad. They'd obviously argued recently, and while Hannah knew it wasn't her fault, she couldn't help but take the girl's mood a little personally. After all, the whole reason Hannah came in the first place was for Abby. She could be eating bagels slathered in cream cheese right now—and wearing sweatpants.

"Y'all go ahead. I'm going to the youth service Sarah told me about." Abby finally spoke up, though she didn't lose her death grip on the children's Bible she held against her side.

"Are you sure? I thought you said your friend Sarah would be out today." Jude's brows furrowed. "You can sit with us. I know it's hard to be new."

"Better there than here." She shot him a meaningful look, full of teenage angst.

Hannah's heart beat a sympathetic rhythm at the

heaviness in Jude's sigh. "All right, go. Meet me in the foyer immediately after." Abby barely had time to scamper down the hallway before Jude called out after her. "Don't be late!"

Abby didn't even award him with a look back.

"I'm sorry." Jude turned back to Sophia and Hannah. "It's been one of those nights—that turned into one of those days. It's not personal." He gestured inside the sanctuary. "Let's go inside. Russell sings in the choir with his wife, but he said he saved us seats on the sixth row."

"Coach Hayes?" Sophia asked in surprise, eyebrows raising.

"He's been going here most of his life. I used to, as well." Jude's gaze locked with Hannah's and he opened his mouth as if to say more, then looked away, obviously unwilling to share more personal details in front of Sophia. "Ladies, after you."

Hannah followed Sophia down the carpeted aisle of the church, lifting her face to drink in the sunlight streaming through the stained glass windows she'd long admired. Depictions of Jesus's life were displayed on each—surrounded by children as He taught the crowds, handing out loaves and fishes to a hungry throng of people, and the Last Supper, surrounded by His closest friends. Despite the scuffling of members settling in the pews and the rustling of bulletins, the church somehow still held a holy quiet, a reverence that seeped into Hannah's soul just as the sunlight seeped into the carpet.

Maybe she had missed this a little.

As she settled into a pew between Sophia and Jude, Hannah's gaze lingered on the stained glass above the pulpit—a beautiful, shimmering cross. She swallowed hard and looked away, unable to handle the emotion of the art, not when everything that once felt so solid about her faith now shook on an unsteady foundation.

"You all right? You look pale."

Hannah turned at Jude's question, low in her ear, and realized too late she'd seated herself on his right side, providing him an unmitigated view of her scarred left cheek.

She ducked her head, fiddling with her bulletin. "I'm fine. It's been a while." She cleared her throat, fighting back the waves of insecurity. She belonged here as much as any other sinner on the pews—the difference was, most of them probably hadn't been shoving God away for the past two years.

Still, hadn't Jude said he'd been away as well? And Sophia had never really been to church at all. What a group they made.

"I apologize for Abby. She really did want you to come." Jude popped his knuckles, a nervous habit. Maybe he felt as unsure inside the church as she did. "Like I said, it's not personal."

"She's almost a teenager." Hannah shrugged. "I didn't take it personally." Not completely, anyway. Well, okay, maybe more than she should have. But she knew better. Teens were teens, and besides,

Hannah had no business trying to force herself into their family unit like she was some sort of missing puzzle piece.

She glanced at Sophia, who had joined in conversation with a woman sitting behind them, and shook her head. Her best friend had never met a stranger. Too bad Hannah couldn't fit into a new environment as easily. Was Abby making friends in the youth room yet? Funny that being borderline snubbed didn't make Hannah any less inclined to worry about the girl.

A knot tied in her stomach. That might be as close to maternal instincts as she'd ever get.

Jude leaned forward, voice low. "Teenager or not, it's no excuse to be rude. She's mad at me, not you."

No big surprise there. Hannah tilted her head, angling it down so her scar would be less intrusive. "What happened?"

"She told me about your fundraiser for CREATE and the art department."

The finality of Jude's tone rang a warning bell in Hannah's mind. "And let me guess. You don't approve." The words slipped out more like a fact than a question, since she didn't need an answer. She'd known that the minute the group decided to model for the magazine. She should have guessed that's what his and Abby's blowout had been about.

"I'm sure you've realized by now that I don't like Abby to be concerned about her appearance—

that includes pictures, and that most certainly includes modeling."

Obviously. But why? "There's nothing wrong with harmless fun in front of a cam—"

"Harmless fun?" Jude interrupted, his hands crumpling his bulletin into a ball. "Modeling isn't harmless. Trust me. I know."

Sophia's words filtered through Hannah's brain, ringing even more alarms. So it was true. Jude's wife used to be a model, and maybe the remains of their marriage had left him with a bad impression of the field. Still, what did that have to do with Abby? Just because her mom had been—or maybe still was—a model didn't mean she'd naturally follow in her footsteps.

Though with her looks, the girl definitely could. Was that what Jude was afraid of?

Hannah laid one arm on Jude's forearm, his muscles bunched underneath the long sleeve of his suit jacket. "I'm sure there's a lot I don't know, and you don't have to tell me. Just please realize it's hard to offer any opinions when I don't have the whole story."

"The whole story?" A muscle worked in Jude's jaw. "That'd take all day. Let me give you the highlights. It starts with two people too young to get married, who did so anyway. One was more beautiful than the other, and she figured it out quickly enough. After a few years of struggling, she realized she could sell those looks to the highest bidder, and have some fun on the side."

"Fun?" Hannah rolled in her lower lip, heart aching at the stony expression on Jude's face. She was almost afraid to ask, but somehow, sensed Jude needed to speak this confession more than she needed to hear it.

Jude lowered his voice even further, casting a quick glance over his shoulder to make sure their conversation was still private. "Drugs. Alcohol. I don't even know the rest." He swallowed, his Adam's apple bobbing, and his next words came out so softly Hannah had to lean sideways to hear. "But I bet there are some other men who do."

Hannah's stomach flipped at the implications. Poor Jude. Then she realized with a start she was still touching his arm. She gave a sympathetic squeeze before slowly removing her hand, shock filling her senses. "I—I don't know what to say. I'm so sorry."

"She's gone now." Jude rubbed the knuckles on the back of his hand, staring as if lost in a different time period. "She died. Overdose, they said. We didn't find out 'til much later." He released his breath. "I don't even know where she's buried."

Hannah stifled a gasp. No wonder he didn't want Abby anywhere near a camera. The memories must be awful to deal with. She couldn't imagine that kind of pain. But still, couldn't he give his daughter a little bit of trust? Abby was a smart kid, and a good one at that. Surely she wouldn't want to become like her mom, even if given the opportunity. If anything, she would be more against drugs and alcohol than a typical teen who hadn't been shown such an ugly part of life.

"Miranda took a lot from us. From our future." Jude's jaw clenched. "I always wanted Abby to have a big family to grow up in, you know? Lots of siblings. I was an only child, was always lonely. I didn't want that for her." He shrugged. "Still don't."

Lots of siblings. Pain pierced Hannah's midsection, and for a moment, the accident was fresh. Raw. On repeat in her head. She closed her eyes against the flashback of images barraging her head and took a deep breath. She was alive. Safe.

But barren.

"Not having any brothers, I'm the last one with my father's name." Jude let out a soft chuckle, void of humor. "So much for carrying out the family tree." He shook his head as piano music began to play from the stage. "I'm sorry. I shouldn't be venting like this. It's— There hasn't been anyone to listen in a long time."

The choir filed into the choir loft on stage, serving as a wake-up cue for Jude.

Embarrassment coated his face, and Hannah wished she could touch him again, offer comfort of some sort to the man who obviously needed to get things off his chest. She could be a friend, even if she never got to be more. And obviously, with the desires he had, she never would. "I'm glad you talked to me. It certainly clears some things up."

"Regardless, I shouldn't have blurted it all out. And at church, no less." Jude carefully unwrinkled his bulletin, laying it flat on his leg and trying in vain to smooth the creases. "But I suppose better to you than to Abby."

Hannah's eyes widened as the music reached a closing crescendo. "You mean Abby doesn't know?" How was that even possible? The girl was almost thirteen years old. Surely she had asked about her mom by now.

Jude stuffed his bulletin in the back of the pew in front of them, beside a hymnal and a community Bible. "She knows her mother is dead, of course. But she doesn't need to know the details of the abandonment beforehand, and that she died of an overdose. It would crush her."

Hannah opened her mouth to argue, but the pain in Jude's eyes looked a lot like the pain Hannah felt on a regular basis—the kind that came with heavy loads of regret and an even bigger dose of "what if." Her judgment toward his decisions softened. Jude knew his daughter better than Hannah did. It wasn't her business to advise him otherwise. So she bit her tongue, and nodded. "I understand."

"I'm glad you do." Relief seeped through Jude's voice, even as the minister of music asked them to stand and join in song. He held the hymnal open for them, lowering his voice to a whisper that hid behind the music. "I need an ally with Abby. Someone who understands my position and will help me keep those boundaries when I'm not there. If you know what I mean…"

She followed his pointed gaze toward Sophia, who was animatedly singing along with her own hymnal.

Hannah raised her eyebrows. "I don't get it."

"At school, and CREATE."

"Are you talking about the magazine?"

At Jude's nod, Hannah frowned. "You mean, you want them to cancel the fundraiser?"

"Not cancel the fundraiser in general. Just persuade them in a different direction." Jude offered a smile, one that could have curled Hannah's toes if she let it go to her head.

But she couldn't get past the disappointment cloaking her heart.

The music around them reached a crescendo. Hannah sang along, trying to keep her expression passive, all while her thoughts churned. She couldn't—*wouldn't*—try to talk them out of the magazine. Not after the kids had gotten so excited. Besides, it was a good idea that would raise money. If the magazine sold, awareness would be raised and the event fundraisers they listed inside, such as the car wash and bake sale, would be better attended and actually have a chance at bringing in bigger bucks later.

Hannah moved her lips, but her voice refused

to join in the happy chorus of praise. She knew—
especially after his confession moments ago—that
Jude had reasons for not loving photography. But
she never thought he'd want to side against the art
department, the very department his own daughter was so passionate about.

She'd been wrong about him.

Maybe he'd been wrong about Hannah after all.

Jude stared at the tiny print in his dusty Bible,
ducking his head to keep Hannah from noticing
the way his gaze kept drawing her direction, over
and over again. Not only did she look fantastic in
blue, her legs encased in knee-high leather boots
that shone the exact color of her dark hair, but she
understood him.

When Jude first shared with her about Miranda,
he wanted to beat himself over the head with the
hymnal for opening his big mouth. Apparently
keeping everything bottled up all the time really
did backfire, as Russell always warned him it
would. But the compassion that radiated in Hannah's expression—not pity, which was all he'd ever
gotten before—struck a chord that resonated deep.

Maybe he'd finally found someone who could
help him with Abby, rather than hinder the way he
was trying to raise her. His parents had been trying
to convince Jude to share the truth with Abby for
years, pressuring him to do things their way rather
than trust that as her dad, he knew best. He would

get this one right. It was too late for Miranda, but not for Abby.

And he'd be hanged if anyone or anything said differently again.

Besides, now that Hannah understood his stand, he could move forward with a proposal to save the sports department and get rid of the drama the art department kept bringing into his home life. If Hannah could use her positive influence on Abby, she'd have no problem trying to talk the CREATE group into a different fundraiser, one inside the parameters he'd set for Abby.

Though he had to admit, from the looks of the budget, any fundraiser at all seemed sort of a moot point. They were talking significant money to keep a department afloat—and a cakewalk just wouldn't cut it.

He cast another glance sideways. Hannah's hair spilled over her scarred cheek as she leaned over her Bible, and once again Jude was struck with the overwhelming desire to brush it with his finger. His initial wondering of her insecurity over the mark had long been confirmed, as she continued to hide the scar with her hair at nearly every turn. Why did it bother her so badly? Sure, it was eye-catching, a definite blemish on an otherwise nearly flawless face, but so were birthmarks or moles or acne. That didn't typically stop someone from hiding themselves from the world by a curtain of hair. Maybe whatever caused the scar—whatever memories surfaced with the reminder—still hurt.

He could relate.

He wished he could wipe it away for her, ease Hannah of the burden it brought—just like she'd helped him carry his burdens today. He couldn't physically remove the scar, but he *could* help her move past it. He'd seen the curious stares from the people in nearby pews, the darting of eyes to and then away from her cheek. Of course she'd noticed as well. How many times had his gaze lingered in that same spot? People meant well, but even still, it had to rub the wrong way.

It was time to show Hannah she was more than a woman with a scar.

The words of the sermon floated unheard past Jude's ears, his thoughts consumed with relief that Hannah understood, and gratitude that tinted dangerously toward affection.

Maybe even something a little more than that.

Chapter Eleven

"I'm sorry about yesterday." Abby's voice chimed so softly, Hannah had to lean over the worktable in order to hear her. "I was in a bad mood at church. But I'm glad you came with us. It really did mean a lot."

Hannah's heart warmed a little at the uncertain smile on Abby's lips, and she patted the girl's shoulder. "I'm glad I came, too." For Abby's sake, anyway. Not for Jude. His plea during the opening worship to cancel the fundraiser sparked a level of indignation deeper than she ever thought she could feel—one that had shocked her into silence. This wasn't her school, this wasn't her job on the line—and these weren't her kids. But somehow, working with this group, especially CREATE, over the past week had opened in her a longing to help, to make a difference, to take a stand.

It was obvious Jude wasn't going to. Did he want the art department to fail? Maybe he was receiving pressure from somewhere else. Sports tended to be more popular than art, but would Jude willingly shoot down his daughter's favorite elective simply because of his own biases? Or was that a bigger issue at stake that Hannah wasn't aware of?

Abby shot Hannah a brighter smile this time, full of gratitude, and resumed flipping the pages of a teen magazine. Sophia had brought a handful of them to CREATE to help the group create a template they liked for their project.

Hannah stared at the glossy pages, but her mind ran in tight circles miles away. The music yesterday had spared her having to answer Jude's absurd request, and after the service, she'd been so overcome by the emotions the sermon and her talk with Jude had dredged up that she turned down Jude's offer of lunch and went home to heat up some soup alone. Even Sophia's plea for a bite to eat at their favorite bistro hadn't tempted her. Being in church had robbed her appetite, serving only as a stark reminder of all the reasons why she quit going in the first place—God was there. She felt Him in the music, saw Him shining through the light in the stained glass windows, heard His voice via the words of the pastor reading the Bible.

But she missed Him deep inside herself, where the hurt seemed to keep multiplying. Would she ever get over her loss? Lots of women were infertile. She wasn't alone, or an oddity. She'd even joined an online community of women like herself to garner support in the months after the accident. Many of them had encouraged her to go back to church, to find comfort in God.

But how she could open herself back up to His presence when He'd abandoned her in her greatest time of need? In the days after the car accident, people had told her she was lucky the only lasting damage was only a scar. They didn't know the worst of it—only her parents, Sophia, and the strangers on the infertility website knew the depth of her tragedy, knew the scars that stretched inside, around her forever-empty womb. They knew the wreck had robbed her of more than just a pretty face. It wasn't something she wanted to broadcast to the world—especially after her fiancé decided he'd rather marry a whole woman, instead of broken pieces. A woman who could provide him with children, someone to carry on the family name.

And wasn't that what all men wanted?

Jude certainly did.

She realized life wasn't over, of course. She could adopt one day—wanted to, even, when the time was right and when she married—if she ever did. But it was one thing to *choose* adoption, another to be robbed of any other options.

"Ms. Hart?" Lana mercifully interrupted her runaway train of thought, and Hannah snapped back to the present. "We like this one." She tapped the magazine that several of the members had gathered around. Even Peter nodded his approval.

"That's a great choice." Hannah spun the magazine around to face her, flipping through the pages splashed with color and text. The format was clean and simple, with plenty of white space to draw the eye, and articles and testimonials from teenagers on each page. The middle of the magazine was a photo layout, showing images of teens in various settings—planting a garden, playing in a pool, eating ice cream at the park. The members of CREATE could easily imitate something similar for their project, and of course, enhance it with their own personal twist.

Sophia joined them at the worktable, taking a break from grading papers, and agreed. "That seems like a good fit for the yearbook committee's program, too. Wouldn't you say, Lana?"

The younger girl nodded proudly as she surveyed the worktable. "That's why I picked it. It seemed familiar."

"Peter, what do you think?" Sophia cast the only boy in the group a quick glance, and Hannah hid her smile. It was just like her friend to care about everyone's opinion, even the ones that might differ from the group and create conflict. She was such a great teacher, making sure everyone had a voice. How could Jude and the board even consider letting someone like Sophia go?

"It looks cool." Peter shoved his hands in his

pockets and nodded slowly, as if he didn't want to show too much excitement. But his eyes sparked with energy. "Not too girlie, you know? But maybe we could use more blue."

The girls groaned, but Hannah broke in. "I'm sure we could change the color scheme to whatever you all preferred. Girls, Peter has a point. This magazine needs to appeal to both girls and guys, for better sales. You have to think marketing."

They murmured reluctant agreements.

"So are we all on the same page?" Hannah asked with a wink. "Pun intended." Heads began to nod, and chatter commenced as the kids began picking out the favorite features of the layout.

"Great!" Sophia clapped her hands to be heard above the sudden din. "Now the real work begins. Peter, why don't you bring those stacks of paper over here from my desk? Everyone, grab a pen. Let's start writing some sample articles for the magazine. Lana, come over here with me and walk me through the yearbook layout program on the computer. We also need to decide how much to charge people for the magazine itself."

"I'll help brainstorm article topics." Hannah pulled out the chair next to Abby just as the school pager system buzzed twice, the signature alarm before an announcement.

"That's weird. School's been out for almost an hour." Sophia frowned as everyone's attention swiveled to the speaker mounted on the wall.

"Attention, attention please." Jude's baritone voice filled the sound waves. "If Hannah Hart is on the premises, will she please report to my office? Hannah Hart to the principal's office."

The system buzzed with a burst of static before the intercom disconnected, leaving a stunned silence to blanket the room.

Hannah's face burned, which she knew only showcased her scar even further. She slowly stood to a chorus of adolescent "oohhs."

"I didn't know teachers could get in trouble," Mya whispered as Hannah pushed her chair in toward the table.

"She's not a real teacher," Peter whispered back as if Hannah wasn't still standing right there. "She's a helper. Like, an aide."

"Still. She should be, like, immune or something."

"Guys, that's enough. Ms. Hart isn't in trouble. Principal Bradley just needs to see her for a minute." Sophia's voice held enough warning to incite the kids back to work. As Hannah passed by her desk, she mouthed, "Tell me everything."

Hannah rolled her eyes at her friend before slipping into the deserted hallway. Her low-heeled shoes echoed through the school like gunshots as she clomped toward Jude's office, wishing she didn't feel like she was going to a duel. Was he going to ask her again to cancel the fundraiser? Why wasn't he asking Sophia about that, instead?

Maybe Hannah's silence yesterday hadn't given him enough of a hint that she disagreed. Then a new thought struck. Surely he didn't think that *because* she didn't answer, she was on board?

She'd find out soon enough.

Hannah pushed inside the office complex, noting Jude's secretary's empty desk, and knocked loudly on his open door. She wasn't about to go into this timid or meek. She couldn't back down, not when the kids she'd grown to love and the dreams they were trying to save lurked right down the hall. Not when her best friend's job was on the line.

Not when participating in CREATE had given her the first selfless thing to focus on in almost two years.

"Great, you're still here!" Jude sprang from his desk, quickly tucking something behind his back before she could see the details. He cleared the chairs in his office and came to stand before her, an almost goofy grin on his face. "I was afraid I'd missed you."

Hannah took a step back, caught off guard at the collapse of his professional armor. Even at church yesterday, while pouring out his heart, Jude had remained proper and professional, the epitome of a businessman. It was who he was. If she'd thought that charm was hard enough to resist, this side of Jude was going to be downright impossible.

She squared her shoulders. Charming or not, she simply didn't agree with him about the art department. And this time, she'd make sure he knew that before he tried to involve her in any more of his schemes. For a man who was so concerned about his daughter's welfare, he sure didn't seem to be that concerned with her happiness. Maybe it wasn't Hannah's business, but it was her choice not to participate in something she felt borderline unethical. "I need to tell you something."

"Sure. Ladies first." Jude gestured with his free hand, one arm still behind his back, but by now Hannah was on too much of a roll to stop and ask why.

She cleared her throat, the image of the kids working back in their elective room spurring on her courage. "I don't know what impression I gave you yesterday at church, but I'm not going to, as you said, *persuade* the CREATE group to think about another project."

The surprise in Jude's eyes gave way to shock, then mild disappointment. Hannah barreled on before her trembling hands could coax her into silence. "This fundraiser is perfect. It provides a way for the students to have fun together *and* use the skills their club has taught them—which is what CREATE is all about in the first place. Taking what they love and making it work in the real world."

Jude opened his mouth, but Hannah railroaded him before he could speak. "I'm truly sorry about your history with your ex-wife, but I don't feel that has anything to do with the art department today." Her resolve strengthened as the words poured out, and her voice rose with energy. "It's serving a purpose for the kids here—especially Abby—and I'm not about to rip it apart from the inside out. I thought you, of all people, would understand that as a parent."

The disappointment in Jude's eyes morphed into a hard glint, and a muscle in his jaw twitched. He adjusted his stance, reminding Hannah of a caged tiger ready to pounce. He looked down briefly, as if attempting to control his temper. All hints of the carefree, happy mood he'd been in moments ago had cleared faster than the school hallways on a Friday afternoon. When he finally spoke, his tone was level, nearly robotic. "Are you finished?"

"With CREATE? No." Hannah crossed her arms over her chest, hands still trembling, and took a deep breath to calm the rush of adrenaline that came with being uncharacteristically aggressive. It felt good to stand up for something she knew was right, felt good finally having a reason to come out of the shell she'd been encased in for the past two years. "But with this conversation, yes." She lifted her chin. "Isn't that why you called me in here, anyway?"

Jude's hand finally came from behind his back, and he thrust a bouquet of pink roses into her arms. "In a word, no."

* * *

"Why did Ms. Hart leave CREATE early today?" Abby asked as she buckled her seat belt.

Jude shrugged as he pulled the car into traffic, hating that once again he couldn't tell Abby the full truth. What could he say? That she'd left out of sheer embarrassment? He changed lanes and slowed down for the coming stoplight. "Maybe she wasn't feeling well."

"Did she look sick when she came to your office?" she persisted.

Sort of. Hannah had certainly turned a rainbow of colors after he handed her those flowers and stalked past her, leaving her in his office as he hightailed it to the men's room to get some distance and control of his emotions. When he'd come out minutes later, she'd been long gone. He half expected to see the flowers in the trash can, but the only sign of them was a single green leaf on the floor in the doorway. Had she kept them?

He'd bought those flowers to put a smile on Hannah's face, had big plans of delivering them with a compliment and a thank-you for accompanying them to church yesterday—and maybe even a request to meet up again the following weekend.

Talk about not going as planned.

Abby twisted in her seat to face him, eyeing him suspiciously. "Ms. Hart was fine when she left to go to your office, but she never came back. Sophia had to bring her purse out to her car for her."

Jude drummed his fingers on the steering wheel. "I really don't know for sure, Abby. Why don't you ask her next week?" Maybe if Abby or the other kids confronted Hannah about her disappearance, she'd have to find some answers and let him off the hook. He had enough ire from his daughter without adding the responsibility of this incident to his list of crimes—besides, today wasn't even his fault. He'd tried to do something nice—Hannah was the one who had stormed inside his office looking for a fight. And what a fight it'd been. He'd never thought someone could look that beautiful while telling him off. She believed in what she said.

Too bad he believed otherwise.

Though as usual, he could have handled his end of things better. A verse from the sermon yesterday, the few pieces he'd heard, anyway, floated through his mind. *A hot-tempered man stirs up strife, but he who is slow to anger quiets contention.* Jude was a poster boy for that particular advertisement. *God, I'm trying now. I really am.* At least he'd gone to the men's room this time instead of raising his voice in return. That was a start.

Or maybe he was truly pathetic.

"Can I call her?" Abby asked. She bent forward and unzipped her purse, as if she was going to pull out her phone and dial her up right then.

"No, not right now." Or ever. Jude steered the car into their driveway, grateful once again for the fact they lived only a few miles from the school.

Lately it seemed the less time he and Abby had to talk in the car, the better. "If she's not feeling well, then she needs some privacy."

Whatever caused Hannah to leave without explanation, she definitely didn't need Abby quizzing her the same afternoon. Jude refused to allow the situation to escalate by Abby getting involved. He threw the gear into Park. "You'll see her at class tomorrow."

"But she doesn't teach us on Tuesdays." Abby pouted.

Jude pulled the keys from the ignition. "You'll still see her soon. Don't worry about it."

Abby didn't look convinced, but thankfully didn't push the issue further as she climbed out of the car. She casually rotated subjects—too casually. "We made great progress on the magazine today."

Jude's hands tightened around his briefcase handle, but he kept his mouth shut as he fumbled with the house key to unlock the door. No temper here. Nope, he was going to open the door and kick off his shoes and find the remote control and not let the magazine get to him—

Abby hitched her backpack on her shoulder, head tilted as she looked up at him. "We're going to start taking pictures for it this weekend."

Now she was baiting him. Jude licked his dry lips, letting Abby inside the house first before he shut the door behind them. He dropped his briefcase on the floor and slid off his loafers, exactly as planned.

"Is that okay?" Her overly confidant voice turned hesitant, and Jude turned to look down into those blue eyes he saw every day in his own reflection. Except Abby's were void of the heavy regret his mirror revealed. What would her gaze hold in ten years? Fifteen? Resentment toward him? Unconditional love? At the rate they were going lately, Jude almost didn't want to know.

"You know how I feel about modeling and vanity." Jude kept his voice low and even as he headed to the kitchen for a drink of water, Abby on his heels. "That hasn't changed."

She dropped her backpack on the floor by the counter. "But Dad, this is for a good cause. I promise I won't get a big head because I'm in a magazine. It's not like I was discovered or something crazy. It's for school."

Jude couldn't stop shaking his head as he filled a glass at the sink.

"Dad. Please?" Abby opened her mouth to argue further, and then paused, as if debating within herself. She finally sighed with great resignation. "I won't even ask to wear makeup or cool clothes. I promise."

Jude shut off the running water with a quick twist of the faucet. If she hadn't been so serious, her compromise would have been comical. But for

Abby, that was a big step—and proved she'd been listening to him over the last several months.

He continued his silent debate in his head as he downed half the glass of water. With Hannah's position now clear—crystal clear—he didn't have the backup to persuade the CREATE team to find a new project, and therefore no way to shut down the magazine idea without looking like a monster. Or without having to tell Abby the truth about her mother.

Maybe CREATE could come through with their fundraisers and spare the school the headache of having to eliminate a department next year. Jude still had to make a proposal, regardless—there wouldn't be time for any money to roll in before the deadline Coleman gave him. But if CREATE could make a dent in the budget with their efforts, maybe the school could put off the inevitable for another semester.

And if not, well—maybe after this attempt, he would know which way to slant the proposal after all.

Jude lowered his glass and met Abby's hopeful expression with a smile. "Okay. You have my permission."

Abby's eyes lit and she jumped against Jude in a tight hug, bumping his arm and sending water all over the floor and the front of his slacks. "Thank you! It'll be fine, I promise. You'll see."

Oh, he'd see, all right. Jude had every intention of being there whenever the CREATE members held their little photo shoot. But we wouldn't spoil Abby's happiness now with those details. He gave her a return hug before grabbing a towel off the counter to clean the spill. "This is a one-time occasion, Abby. Remember that. My rules haven't changed."

Abby scooped up her backpack with a grin. "I know!" She turned and fairly floated down the hall to her room.

Jude sat back on his heels and watched her go, wet towel in hand. Somehow, he didn't think she knew at all.

Chapter Twelve

"Abby, are you sure your dad agreed to let you go to the photo shoot tomorrow?" Hannah planted her hands on her hips and gave Abby her best school-teacher stare—one she'd perfected over the last few weeks by watching Sophia. She didn't even bother to keep her voice down, as Sophia and the rest of the kids had already left for the afternoon. The last CREATE meeting of the week had ended, and on a highly productive note as the fundraiser magazine progressed nicely.

Hannah had promised to stay with the dawdling Abby and lock up the elective classroom when the girl finally got her belongings together—or rather, *if* she ever did. If Abby wasn't fighting with her dad anymore, then why the obvious stalling and lingering in the bathroom at the end of the meeting, then organizing her pencil case and painstakingly throwing away small pieces of paper from her bag?

"Of course he did. I wouldn't lie." Abby barely looked up from carefully uncapping and recapping all of her pens.

Hannah tilted her head, studying Abby across the work table laden with rough drafts of the magazine. Working with the kids several times a week, both in Sophia's art class and twice a week at CREATE, had revealed to Hannah a couple of their individual tells. For instance, if Peter was going along with something he didn't really like in order to avoid being fussed at by five girls, he licked his lips before reluctantly agreeing. If Lana was struggling with not getting her way, she twisted her hair around her finger in rapid motion.

And when Abby was up to her schemes, she avoided eye contact.

Hannah crossed her arms. "I'm not calling you a liar, but I have a hard time believing he changed his mind so easily." Especially after the fit Hannah threw. In fact, she'd been surprised Jude hadn't insisted she leave the school premises immediately after she burst into his office earlier in the week. After he'd handed the flowers to her and stalked out of the room, Hannah had stood in his office, shocked at both herself and Jude, the sweet aroma of roses a stark contradiction to the bad taste of regret filling her mouth.

That was Monday, and she hadn't seen him since. Was he avoiding her? Of course, if he was, she'd made it easy, slipping into the school via the back door, bypassing the teachers' lounge and the office complex by taking the long way through the building.

Abby finally zipped her backpack. "I thought the same thing about my dad changing his mind, but trust me, it wasn't easy." She shouldered her bag, lifting her ponytail so as not to snag her long hair on the straps. "I had to convince him—and promise not to wear makeup or any borrowed cool clothes." She rolled her eyes with the practiced angst of a teenager. "But it will be worth it."

"I agree." Hannah ushered Abby toward the hall, flipping off the lights and making sure the classroom door locked behind them. "It's worth it to know you played a part in helping save the art department."

"Do you really think our fundraisers will work?" Abby cast a hopeful gaze at Hannah as they made their way through the deserted school to the parking lot.

It'd take a lot of sales of the magazine, as well as significant participation in the fundraisers they were advertising, to make any sort of real difference. But Hannah couldn't disappoint the girl this early in the game with those negative odds.

She chose her words carefully, determined not to lie. "I think if we work hard, then nothing is impossible." Maybe not likely, but not impossible, either. Maybe the "not likely" part was what Jude was counting on.

"The youth pastor at church Sunday said the same thing." Abby adjusted her bag on her back. "He said nothing is impossible with God."

"That's true." True, though harder to accept. If God could do anything, why didn't He protect Hannah's womb from irreparable damage? Why didn't He protect her face from the scar that would mock her the rest of her life?

Why didn't He keep her from developing feelings for a man she could never have?

Hannah glanced over her shoulder, hoping she wouldn't run into Jude while he waited for Abby. Maybe he was already in the parking lot—in which case, she needed to hurry.

She hesitated at the front doors of the school. "Have a good night, Abby. I'll see you tomorrow at the photo shoot."

"Wait!" Abby touched Hannah's arm. "I, uh—sort of need a ride." She offered a sheepish grin.

"Why didn't you say something sooner?" Hannah scanned the parking lot through the window, which was indeed void of cars besides Hannah's SUV. "Where's your dad?"

"He had a meeting off campus. So I told him I'd get a ride, rather than missing CREATE." Abby pushed her way outside, leaving Hannah no choice but to follow.

"Abby, you should have asked me earlier. What if you had ended up stuck here alone?" Thankfully Hannah didn't have any pressing appointments this evening. She led Abby to her car and unlocked the doors.

"I'm sorry, I guess I forgot." Abby avoided eye contact again, hesitating before climbing onto the passenger seat. "Do you mind?"

"No, it's fine. Just ask sooner next time, okay? I'd hate for you to get stranded. Your dad wouldn't like that, either." To put it mildly. Somehow it'd probably become Hannah's fault if she had. But that wasn't fair. Jude had never been unfairly accusatory. In fact, if he hadn't brought up the whole concept of changing the fundraiser, those flowers would have been sweet.

And incredibly welcome.

But there was no changing anything now. Besides, the flowers could have meant something different. She was reading way too much into a couple of blooms and leaves she'd stashed in a vase in her town house—then hid in the corner of the kitchen because of the guilt that came every time she saw them.

"Sweet ride." Abby buckled her seat belt as Hannah started the ignition, then ran her hand over the arm rest. "I told dad he should have gotten an SUV a few years ago, but he said they aren't practical. He calls them gas-guzzlers." She rolled her eyes again, and Hannah hid her smile.

"They can be expensive, but I needed something big enough to haul around my photography props and equipment." High gas prices or not,

Hannah would never own a compact car again—not after the way hers had nearly taken her life in that wreck.

Hannah brushed aside the memories that still made her drive with a tighter grip on the steering wheel than necessary. "Where to? Your house?"

"No." Abby offered the same sheepish expression from before. "Dad and I had plans to eat pizza for dinner tonight after his meeting. So...Mario's?"

Hannah flipped on her blinker and turned onto the main road, unsure if it was her place to lecture Abby on being more responsible. But she'd already explained the importance of not waiting until the last minute, so that was enough for one day. Still, the sooner she dropped Abby off and got back home, the better—hopefully without having to see Jude. She'd have to face him eventually, but preferably not today. Or tomorrow.

Or the next week.

A few minutes later, Hannah parked outside Mario's Pizza Pavilion, the best pizza in town, and tried to ignore the way her stomach growled at the very thought of cheese and greasy pepperoni. "Here we are. See you tomorrow."

"Aren't you coming in?" Abby slid outside and hiked her backpack on her shoulder, eyes pleading. "You were the one who said it was important not to get stranded somewhere alone. What if Dad isn't here yet?"

She had said that, hadn't she? Abby might be

almost thirteen, but Hannah couldn't send her inside, sight unseen, not knowing if she was safe. With a sigh, Hannah turned off the engine and followed Abby inside.

The smell of bell peppers, sausage and mozzarella assaulted Hannah's senses and sent her mouth to watering. She glanced around the crowded red booths for Jude, and with a dip of her heart, spotted him in the back by the arcade games. She licked her dry lips, and pushed Abby ahead of her. "There he is, sweetie. I'd better go."

"What? You have to stay and eat!" Abby tugged Hannah along, weaving past the maze of tables toward the back. "I'll even pay for your pizza out of my allowance. It's the least I can do after making you give me a ride."

"Abby, that's sweet but really, it's not necessary." Hannah tried to pull away, but by then, Jude had seen them approaching, and it would have caused a scene to slip back outside.

"Hannah." Jude's voice filled with surprise, and he stood as they arrived at the booth. "What are you doing here?"

She was wondering the same thing. Hannah drew a deep breath and pushed her hair back from her eyes. "I gave Abby a ride." She kept her voice level, though part of her wanted to collapse with embarrassment and part of her still smoldered that he'd taken off his Principal hat long enough to bring her flowers in the first place. What kind of game was he playing anyway?

Yet another, even smaller part—the part that enjoyed romance novels and long bubble baths and walks on the beach—wished he'd buy her another bouquet and give her a second chance.

"Can we get two pizzas this time?" Abby slid into the booth where Jude had sat, seemingly oblivious to the tension between the two adults.

Jude's eyes narrowed, ignoring her question. "I thought you said Lana's mom was giving you a ride."

"They had to leave." Abby stared intently at the menu in her hands—which was upside down.

"You should have called me, then. Ms. Hart shouldn't have had to do that." Jude briefly closed his eyes, then motioned for Hannah to sit on the other side of the table. "Please, join us. Buying you dinner is the least we can do for your trouble."

"That's what I said." Abby looked up with a beaming smile, before catching her father's furrowed brow and burying her face back into the menu.

Hannah slowly slid into the vacant seat across from Abby, wishing there was a graceful way out of this cozy little scenario. Well, if she was here, she might as well enjoy the free meal and make the best of it. She decided to take Abby's preferred method of evasion, and scooped up her own menu. "Do you guys come here a lot?"

"It's our favorite." Abby tapped her dad's arm. "I want sausage, okay? No mushrooms." She began pushing Jude out of the booth. "I'm going to go play Pac-Man."

With a sigh, Jude let her out before reclaiming the vinyl seat. He leaned back with a soft laugh. "I'm really sorry you got caught up in this. I know you didn't— Well, you weren't—"

"Wanting to see you?" Hannah surprised even herself with the sassy retort, and clenched her menu in both hands. But she didn't want to shy away, didn't want to leave the awkwardness between them unresolved. For Abby's sake, of course.

But even that excuse was wearing thin.

Amusement lit Jude's eyes, along with a sheen of admiration. "Something like that, yes."

"Let's just say you aren't the only one who can lose their temper." Hannah traced the rim of the menu with her finger, wishing she didn't have to make eye contact and lose herself in the what-ifs of his electric-blue gaze. "I'm sorry for storming your office like I did. I was on a mission—an unnecessary one, obviously."

"No, I'm the one who's sorry. I had it coming." Jude reached across the table and snagged the red pepper shaker, as if he, too, needed something to occupy his hands. "And regardless, I shouldn't have gotten upset and left."

"It wasn't very professional of me, either, coming

in like that. Especially because of—" Hannah cleared her throat. "Because of the flowers."

"You didn't know." A hint of red tinged Jude's cheeks, and a rush of relief that he was a little embarrassed by the gesture as well filled Hannah's stomach. "I hadn't exactly given you fair warning."

Warning? Of what—his feelings for her? Or were the flowers simply an apology for his absurd request for her help with shutting down the fundraiser?

She opened her mouth, needing to find out, wanting to know the truth before she made yet another faux pas, but the waitress came to take their order and the moment was lost.

When the waitress brought their drinks and left, Jude leaned forward, resting his forearms on the table. "Thanks for giving Abby a ride. I think she's up to her old tricks."

"What kind of tricks?" Hannah slid her menu back into place in the holder against the wall, then smiled as Abby's delighted laugh, mixed with the telltale electronic beeps of the arcade game, sounded over the back of the booth. At least someone was having fun.

Though come to think of it, she couldn't remember why she was supposed to be mad at Jude—especially after their mutual apology. Maybe they could start fresh.

Maybe those flowers could mean what she hoped they did.

"Her matchmaking tricks." Jude shook his head, turning to look back at Abby playing. "Telling you she needed a ride here while telling me her friend was dropping her off."

Hannah's eyes widened. No wonder Abby had been stalling so long after school. She'd been making sure there was no one else to take her to Mario's besides Hannah. Pretty sneaky—and genius, come to think of it. But why did she want to set Hannah up with her dad? Did she want Hannah in her life that much? The thought warmed her insides, soothing her internal scars like a gentle balm. She might not ever get to be a real mother one day, but little moments like this—being chosen by a child—felt almost as good.

She could get used to this—and in more ways than one. Her stomach fluttered at Jude's proximity, at the way his carefully gelled hair drooped a little at the end of the day, at the way the muscles in his forearms flexed as he absently ripped paper off a straw.

Hannah's thoughts drifted into dangerous territory. What would it be like to be a part of a real family—meeting up for pizza after a long day, finding quarters for arcade games, passing around napkins, laughing over inside jokes only a close family unit would understand. Would she ever get the chance to find out?

And more important—would she get to find out *with* Jude and Abby?

Jude twirled the straw in his soda cup, the clanking of ice cubes breaking her daydream. "Abby's done this before—tried to set me up with different teachers or women in her life."

Hannah's mouth dried. So she wasn't chosen after all. Her heart plummeted to the floor of the booth and she stared at her chipped manicure, trying in vain to push back the emotion that threatened to overcome. Not chosen by Abby—and definitely not by Jude.

Jude rambled on about Abby's previous matchmaking schemes, but she stopped listening, keeping her gaze riveted on a crack in the Formica table. It wasn't that Hannah expected a man like Jude to never date, but from the impression he gave, romance wasn't his top priority. He'd made that clear over the course of their interactions. Was that true with everyone, or just her? Had he turned down Abby's other matchmaking attempts over the years—or only this one?

She swallowed, her appetite for pizza suddenly gone. Obviously the flowers weren't a special gesture on Jude's part, after all—they probably represented the apology she'd first imagined. One of Pecan Grove's most eligible bachelors, who used to be married to a model, wouldn't be interested in someone like Hannah. Why did she keep forgetting that and allowing herself to hope? Maybe Abby, in her childlike innocence, could look past Hannah's scar and not be ashamed, but a professional like Jude, climbing the career ladder in the school, needed someone at his side who wasn't afraid to face the public. Someone who wasn't content to hide behind her camera.

Someone who could give him siblings for Abby one day.

Hannah shifted uncomfortably in the booth and rubbed her arms with both hands, suddenly chilled despite the heat from the brick ovens in the nearby kitchen.

Would she ever be someone's first choice?

Jude bit into an extra cheesy piece of pizza, eyeing Hannah across the table as she delicately nibbled on her own slice of pepperoni. What happened? One minute they were apologizing and chatting amicably about Abby, and the next minute Hannah shut down. The woman ran hot and cold more than anyone he'd ever met—literally, by the way she kept rubbing her arms riddled with goose bumps. Was it something he said? He thought back over the previous conversation, but nothing jumped out at him as offensive or antagonistic.

He wiped his fingers on a napkin, thoughts churning. Women. It seemed the ones in his recent experience were all after either a good time with no commitment attached, or money.

The first he refused to offer, the second he couldn't.

Thankfully, Abby broke the tension hovering

over their table with meaningless chitchat about her friends at school, her woes over math, and the ridiculous amount of history homework she had over the weekend. Which reminded Jude—he still hadn't told Abby he was tagging along to the photo shoot tomorrow. Maybe dropping that proverbial bomb would be less explosive if he did so in front of Hannah. Abby knew she had already crossed a line with her little scheme for getting a ride earlier, so hopefully she would take the information in stride and not embarrass either one of them.

Hopefully.

Jude cleared his throat, breaking into Abby's endless stream of chatter. "You ready for tomorrow's photo shoot?"

His daughter's eyes widened, and even Hannah looked up from the straw wrapper she'd been meticulously folding into sixteenths. What? Did they think him such an ogre that he couldn't even discuss things he disagreed about with them?

Abby took a long sip of her Sprite before answering. "I think so." She darted a glance at Hannah, then back at Jude.

He casually plucked another slice of pizza from the pan in the middle of the table. "I can't wait to see how it goes."

Abby sputtered, nearly choking as she set her cup down. Sprite dripped down the front of her flowered top. "What do you mean?"

Hannah handed her a few napkins, frowning as

her eyes darted back and forth between Abby and Jude. Oh, so now he had her full attention—for the first time in twenty minutes.

He shrugged, focusing on his pizza, still playing it cool. "I thought I'd tag along." There really was no *thinking* about it, either he was going or Abby wasn't. But he'd give her a chance to save face instead of flinging more rules at her. They'd made such progress with their compromise the other day, he hated to ruin the camaraderie they'd managed ever since. "That's all right with you, isn't it?"

Abby's face paled and she shot Hannah a pleading look, but Hannah only shrugged. Abby raised her eyebrows, and Hannah shook her head, almost imperceptibly. Abby bit her lower lip.

Jude watched the exchange, tension creeping up his shoulders. What was this, some sort of silent conversation in girl-code? He couldn't have done that with Abby if he'd tried. No wonder Hannah had all but laughed in his face when he asked if she knew of any tricks for communicating better.

He'd have to start wearing pantyhose and curlers in his hair to have a chance.

Abby let out a resigned sigh. "I guess so." Then the table bumped as if someone had kicked their leg out, and Abby jumped slightly. "I mean, yes. Totally fine."

Jude's gaze flicked to Hannah, whose expression remained a little *too* nonchalant. He tried to hide his shock—and jealousy at her successful methods of dealing with his hormonal daughter—as he stirred the ice in his glass. "Great. Then it's settled."

Nope. He didn't have a chance at all.

Chapter Thirteen

The sun released a morning's worth of red streaks into the sky, highlighting the sketchy cloud cover and turning the puffy white mounds to amber. Hannah drew a deep breath of the cool autumn air, grateful she'd worn a hoodie over her long-sleeved shirt. Downtown Pecan Grove still slumbered, most of the offices closed for the weekend. But the multi-story buildings, the red-striped awning in front of the town's most popular bakery, and the abandoned railroad tracks would make great backdrops. The lighting would be perfect once the clouds broke a little—that is, assuming the kids woke up enough to actually take photos.

She turned to face Sophia, who had converted the hatchback of Hannah's SUV into a mini breakfast station for the students, and couldn't help but laugh as her friend rolled her eyes. The kids were leaning against the side of the car and even each other, bleary-eyed and munching donuts like zombies, while the fruit tray nestled beside the gallon of orange juice went ignored.

Hannah gestured to the food stash. "It was a good try." She plucked a handful of grapes from the tray and popped them into her mouth, one by one. "Short of giving them coffee, there's not much else we can do."

Sophia reached for a strawberry, then changed her mind and grabbed a donut covered in sprinkles instead. "Maybe they'll perk up when everyone is here and we start working. We're still waiting on Abby."

Hannah cast a quick glance around the parking lot, void of cars except for hers and Sophia's and an early-rising business owner or two. The other parents had dropped their kids off and headed away, Starbucks in hand, grateful for the rare Saturday morning free time. Had Jude changed his mind and kept Abby home? Or had they simply overslept? After last night's awkward conversation over pizza, Hannah could believe either scenario.

She closed her eyes against the memories of yesterday evening, grateful for the happy moments, yet regretting them at the same time. It'd been too easy to imagine herself a part of their family. She'd hoped for it, and gotten disappointed when reality reared its all-too-familiar and ugly head. Was it just that she wanted to belong to someone, anyone? Or to Jude and Abby specifically?

Hannah opened her eyes as tires crunched in the

gravel parking lot, her heart leaping a traitorous beat as Jude parked beside her SUV.

There was her answer.

Sophia wiped a sprinkle from her cheek. "Finally." She clapped her hands, trying to rouse the kids. "Lana, Mya, Peter. Let's go. Tiffany, hand Ms. Hart her bag, please. Rachel, can you help with that basket of props?"

Hannah stood silently as the kids scurried into motion, watching as Jude and Abby climbed out of the car. She fingered the thick strap around her neck, grateful for the comforting armor her camera provided. She'd be the one behind the camera today—though Jude probably wished the same for Abby.

Was he going to handle things all right? She still couldn't believe he had chosen to keep the truth about his ex-wife's death secret from his daughter. Had he told others, or had Hannah been a rare confidant that Sunday in church?

Her thoughts flickered to the other matchmaking attempts he said Abby had made over the years, and a slow burn she could only describe as jealousy filled her stomach. At this rate, the sooner she could finish her stint with Sophia's art class and CREATE, and get back to her regular routine, the better. When it came to Jude, she kept forgetting who she was.

And who she'd never be.

"Good morning." Hannah forced what she hoped

appeared to be a casual smile as the father-daughter duo approached, nervously dunking her hands in the front pockets of her hoodie. How could a man look so good so early in the day?

"Good morning," Abby echoed, covering a yawn with her hand. She ran her fingers absently through her long hair, free of its typical braid. She must have won a battle with her hair, though not with her clothes. While the other girls had come in designer jeans or knee-length flouncy skirts with boots and sweaters with sparkly threads, Abby wore a simple denim sheath dress buttoned to the top—without a single accessory to brighten the simple color.

Hannah nibbled her lower lip. While she understood Jude's drive for conservatism and modesty, Abby would look out of place in the pictures, standing out in a way that surely even Jude wouldn't want for her. The other girls' sparkle and color would leave Abby left out. Could he not understand that? Most single dads weren't very fashion conscious, but Abby was like a walking page from a children's magazine, prompting kids to find obvious differences. It wouldn't be fair. But what could she do, knowing his stand on the issue?

"There's donuts and juice over there." Jude's deep voice broke through Hannah's thoughts, making her stomach dip. He sounded good first thing in the morning, too. She tried to steady her pulse, reprimanding herself for her reaction to his presence. Jude was Abby's dad, and her temporary boss of sorts. Just because they shared an outing for pizza in a family-type setting didn't mean his feelings for her had changed, or that the flowers he'd given her meant anything other than gratitude.

Or worse, pity.

Jude steered Abby toward the refreshments. "Go ahead and eat and wake up." He smiled as Abby drifted toward the other kids, grunting greetings as they carried out the tasks Sophia had assigned. "She's not exactly an early riser."

Hannah nodded. "I wasn't, either, but had to get used to it over the years. Have to capture the best light and all." She tapped her camera, unable to help but notice the tightness in Jude's jaw. He shoved his hands in his pants pockets and rocked back on his heels, eyes skipping over the kids as they darted around with props and camera bags, following Sophia's commands. Was he realizing the difference between Abby and the others? Did he care, or was that what he wanted?

"We're ready." Sophia hustled toward Hannah, a big folded blanket in her arms. "Which backdrop should we shoot first?"

Hannah forced her mind off Jude, letting thoughts of his discomfort fade to the background of her mind even as he edged into the background of her vision, separating himself from the chaos. "Let's head to the bakery. Someone grab that last box of donuts."

Peter scooped it up and the kids traipsed after

Hannah and Sophia toward the red-striped awning. Hannah arranged the scene, handing each kid a donut and giving instructions on eating and laughing while pulling them apart with their fingers. "Mya, you and Lana stand here by the pole. Face each other and act like you're telling secrets. Good. Now, Peter, you sneak up on them from behind and pretend to throw your donut—no, Peter. *Pretend*."

The girls squealed as they picked sugar crumbs out of their hair, and Sophia snorted back a laugh. "You should have seen that one coming."

Click. The scene was perfect though, the candidness of the moment shining through. She took another, then instructed the remaining girls to pose in various places around the bakery.

Hannah cast a quick glance over her shoulder at Jude, who scrubbed the sidewalk with the toe of his shoe, looking as if he'd rather be anywhere else in the world. Why had he come, if he knew he'd be miserable? Did he not trust Abby with her and Sophia? She shook her head. No time to worry about that now. And again—it didn't matter.

Even if her heart had yet to catch up to that fact.

Hannah clapped her hands as Sophia typically did, garnering attention. "Great job, guys! Take ten." She gave the kids a quick water break while reviewing some of the previous photos, wincing at Abby's appearance. What seemed obvious enough in person came across as downright stark on film. The overlying goal of the photo shoot might be for the fundraiser, but that didn't mean Abby should be embarrassed in the process. Hannah wished she could help—but she couldn't, not without deliberating going against Jude's wishes.

Like it or not, as he made clear over and over—she wasn't a parent.

"Abby! Come here!"

Hannah glanced up from her camera as Lana hollered for Abby to join her in the parking lot, where the girls had left their purses in the hatchback of the SUV. Abby jogged toward her friend, and Lana pulled a gauzy green scarf from her oversized bag. She wrapped the scarf around the Abby's neck, and adjusted the ties to hang down the front of her dress. Then she handed Abby something smaller, which she immediately put on her wrist. Bangles. Hannah couldn't hear the words they exchanged, but the hug Abby gave her friend said plenty.

Hannah turned off the review feature on her camera and grinned. Lana had done what Hannah couldn't, and unless Jude wanted to make a scene over a simple scarf, the problem was solved. Perfect.

"You look cute," Hannah whispered to Abby as she girl strolled back past her toward their makeshift set. Abby threw her a grateful smile, even more brilliant against the deep green of the scarf, and shook her bangles appreciatively.

Hannah arranged the next scene, and at Mya's

suggestion, Abby gathered all of her hair to one side and draped it over her shoulder. The silky blond strands popped against the green scarf and lit Abby's eyes better than any makeup product could have. Hannah smiled. Beautiful. Now, she would fit in.

Just hopefully not at the expense of her dad's approval.

Jude joined the students from his jaunt across the parking lot for a water bottle, just as the next photo session wrapped up. His eyes sought out his daughter, then blinked twice at her transformation. Was she wearing makeup?

He squinted, fighting the natural rise of his blood pressure, then relaxed. No, the green scarf near her face just made her complexion shine. That and some bracelets dangling on her wrist was all that had changed. But still—if he'd wanted Abby to wear all that mess, he'd have let her put it on before leaving the house. Before, she'd looked simple. Smart. Modest.

Now she looked like the other girls.

He drew a deep breath, trying to remember the Bible verses he'd read about anger, trying to remind himself that Abby wasn't Miranda. A scarf wasn't implants and bracelets weren't diet pills. This meant nothing.

He kept his mouth shut and leaned against the side of a brick building, arms crossed, while

Hannah arranged the group around their next back-drop—the railroad tracks long abandoned that ran through the perimeter of downtown Pecan Grove. Abby and the others balanced atop the rails, arms out, laughing and wobbling and holding on to each other for balance. Hannah clicked away while Sophia stood nearby, occasionally stepping in to adjust someone's hair or hand over a prop, such as a textbook or a backpack.

Despite his aversion to her career, Jude couldn't help but admire Hannah's ease behind the camera. She transformed from a reserved, timid individual into a woman with a passion who knew what she was doing. It was as if she forgot about her scar, forgot her inhibitions, and let the true Hannah shine through the lens. The kids responded to her easy, carefree manner as well, and even Jude could tell from this distance that the shots would be great. The students were having fun and using their newly acquired skills from class. Hannah even let a few of them carefully take pictures with her camera, posing each other and acting as professional photographers. Who else would trust a bunch of junior high students with expensive equipment? Jude truly enjoyed seeing this side of Hannah—and wished he could be the one to coax her out of her shell.

Once again, he was bested by a camera.

Jude shifted positions against the rough building. He had no business thinking of Hannah that way. Maybe the bad timing with the flowers had been a sign of some sort, a warning not to get involved over his head. He didn't deserve someone like Hannah, someone so sweet and beautiful. He'd messed up that kind of innocence before with neglect, and he couldn't—wouldn't—give himself the opportunity to do it again. Not to a second wife, and definitely not to his daughter.

The bricks pressed against his back, rough and cool. He wanted to marry again, eventually—after all, he didn't want to be alone forever after Abby grew up and went to college, got married herself.

But everything about Hannah Hart screamed complicated.

What had he been thinking, wanting to go there with the flowers? Hannah might be beautiful—and sweet, and generous and devoted to the things she cared for—but that devotion was what made him nervous. After all, she'd stood up to him multiple times. Proved she wouldn't cater to someone else's suggestions or ideas if she strongly disagreed, even if that someone was in the position of authority like himself.

Yep. Way too complicated.

"Let's take some individual shots for the staff pages." Hannah took the cap back off her camera and said something else to Sophia, the latter words carried away by a gust of wind. Sophia plucked Abby from the group awaiting instructions and brought her to the blanket they'd folded on the ground.

Jude's muscles tensed, and he straightened. Just a picture. It was for the magazine. The fundraiser. A school project. Yet the reminders did little to ease the knot in his stomach as Abby settled on the blanket, crossed her legs and beamed for the camera. In fact, the knot tightened with every click of the shutter, with every toss of Abby's hair and flash of silver jewelry from her wrist.

Wasn't this how it started—baby steps? Inching down a bad path—inches that led to feet that led to yards and then miles. Hadn't Miranda said when she called that modeling agency the first time that she was only playing around? Hadn't she told him that her professional head shots were just in case? That she'd never get discovered or make it big, and that she didn't really want to anyway?

If only Jude had spoken up, he could have spared them all. If he'd been the husband she'd needed, Miranda wouldn't have sought that kind of attention outside of their home. She'd be here now, alive and well, raising Abby and driving the carpool, drug-free and happy with laugh lines creasing her face and freckles dotting her cheeks and not caring in the least. It was all his fault.

He couldn't watch this.

Jude stalked toward Abby, not wanting to make a scene but unable to stay another moment and tolerate what was playing out before him. His hands shook as he drew nearer the private shoot, and he wished he could grab Abby off the blanket, buckle her in the car like a little kid and keep her safe from the world for the rest of her life. Safe from bad influences, safe from bad vices. Safe from the darkness that could so easily consume one's life without warning.

"Dad, what's wrong?" Abby stood up as he approached, and Jude struggled to control the emotions he knew played out on his face.

With great restraint, he kept his voice level. "We're leaving."

"Now? But we're not done." Abby shot Hannah a panicked expression, but Hannah's gaze remained riveted on Jude. She could see straight through him, and that unnerved him almost as much as the fact that his daughter was involved in a modeling session after all his efforts over the years for the exact opposite.

He opened his mouth to argue with Abby, but Hannah jumped in. "I'd be happy to take her home when we're done."

He pressed his lips together, ready to argue and demand Abby leave with him now, when his daughter's pleading gaze caught his.

He almost couldn't bear it. He needed to get away from this whole scene, *now,* before the memories of Miranda and her photo shoots consumed him and made him overreact even further than he already was. Despite him knowing better, the images wouldn't stop parading through his mind. Jude, in the background of a brightly lit studio, rocking Abby to sleep while Miranda pranced around onstage in a swimsuit. Jude feeding Abby a bottle while Miranda posed for cameras, knowing his child shouldn't be there, yet unable to stomach the idea of his wife there alone. Jude, coaxing toddler-Abby to quit crying as Miranda left the house once again for an out-of-town shoot.

Then getting the letter and death certificate in the mail that rocked his world one final time.

"Fine. I'll see you at the house." He turned toward the parking lot, ignoring the whispers that sounded behind his back. He kept walking, facing forward, trying to ignore what lay behind.

But only seeing the past in vivid Technicolor.

Chapter Fourteen

❧

"I hope he's not mad." Abby peered at her house, but made no move to open the door of Hannah's SUV.

Hannah didn't blame her. She slowly shifted the car into Park, unsure what to say. She could calm Abby's fears, but it might be a lie. Hannah had no idea how Jude would react when Abby went inside, had no clue if the two hours that had passed since he left the photo shoot had been enough time for him to get over whatever triggered his bad mood. But it wasn't anger she'd seen in Jude's eyes when he approached her and Abby on the blanket. It'd been something else. Something deeper, stronger. Vulnerable.

Painful.

"Will you go in with me?" Abby looked up at Hannah, eyes honest and sincere, and Hannah hated to tell her no. But it'd be even more awkward for Hannah to crash what would surely be a

father-daughter talk over his sudden departure. Too
bad he wouldn't tell Abby the real truth about her
mom. If he could tell Hannah on a Sunday morning without self-destructing, then surely he could
give his daughter the facts she deserved.

Then another thought struck.

What if Jude wasn't emotionally over his ex-
wife? What if the reason he kept the bitterness so
close and refused to talk to Abby was because it
still hurt him too badly? Maybe he wasn't angry
with his ex after all.

Maybe he was still in love.

"I'm sure you'll be fine, Abby." Hannah fiddled
with the keys dangling in the ignition, wishing
she'd never gotten involved.

But knowing in her heart she'd never had a
choice.

"If you come with me, maybe he'll be in a better
mood." Abby tilted her head, studying Hannah.
"He likes you."

Oh, to be a naive preteen again. "That's sweet,
Abby, but I don't think so. Not in the way you
mean." Never in the way she meant. Not Jude.

Not her.

"How do you know?" Abby crossed her arms,
brow furrowed. "Trust me, I know my dad. And—"

Hannah broke in. "He told me you like to play
matchmaker with him and your other teachers."
She hoped her gentle tone removed some of the
harshness from her words. But if the younger girl

was determined to meddle with adults' feelings, she had to learn what was appropriate. "I know that's fun, but that won't work here." Unfortunately. She absently touched the scar on her cheek, wishing things were different.

A lot of things.

"I don't believe you." Abby grinned and unbuckled her seat belt. "Come on, let's go inside. I'll prove it." She climbed out of the car before Hannah could argue.

"Abby—" The slamming passenger door cut her off, and Hannah reluctantly tugged free of her seat belt. She couldn't let the girl run inside, blurting out who knew what. If Abby wanted to distract Jude from a potential lecture about today's shoot, this topic would certainly do the trick. But that wasn't a price Hannah was willing to pay. She trotted after Abby, who slid to a stop right inside the front door.

"Dad?" Her voice grew timid, not at all confident as it'd been moments ago.

Hannah peered around Abby at Jude, who sat on the couch surrounded by open albums. Scrapbooks. There must have been half a dozen. Though most of the books were upside down, she could easily see photo after photo of a young blonde woman who strongly favored Abby.

Her mom.

Hannah's throat tightened and she tried to look away, but her eyes were drawn like a magnet to the images before her. Professional head shots in a studio. Modeling photos. Full-length pictures from the beach.

The woman really had been perfect.

The scar on Hannah's face tingled, and she ducked her head, covering the blemish, wishing her hair could cover her embarrassment as easily. Why did she care so much about Jude's ex? Why was she comparing herself to this blonde beauty she'd never even met?

Why hadn't she stayed in the car?

Her earlier ponderings now proved true. Why would Jude be perusing old photos, opening old wounds, if he didn't have strong feelings for her, didn't miss her and wish for what once was? No wonder he'd turned down all the matchmaking attempts over the years, and didn't date much. He was still tied to the past.

Jude looked up, then slowly shut the red leather binder in his lap and stood, his face grave. "Abby, we need to talk."

He hadn't seen this coming, though it was about eight years in the making.

"Sit down, Abby." Jude's words directed his daughter, but his eyes locked with Hannah, who ducked her head to hide behind her hair. Why the sudden cover-up? She hadn't done that hair move once at the photo shoot earlier today.

The shoot that apparently caused a lot more drama than he'd realized.

Abby crept forward, her expression wary, and he didn't blame her. This wasn't going to go well, especially since he'd kept the majority of these photo albums—Miranda's glory days—hidden from her over the years.

"I'm going to go." Hannah edged toward the door, eyes flickering back and forth from him to Abby, as if uncertain his daughter would be okay. He wasn't entirely sure himself. Part of Jude wished Hannah would stay and be a neutral territory for Abby after she heard the news he wasn't sure he could actually push through his lips. He could use a Switzerland right about now. But it wasn't fair to ask that of Hannah. He didn't have the right.

Not that the facts changed anything. He didn't have the right to brush her hair back from her face and tell her to quit hiding her scar, but he wanted to do that, too. Wanted to skim her cheek with his fingers, tell her she was more beautiful than she knew. Tell her that despite his earlier resolutions toward her, she was a prize, that her assertiveness over his kid endeared her to him as much as it frustrated him—maybe more.

And that scared him.

No, even if Hannah might actually be what he needed, he would never be what she needed. She might be a prize, but one destined for another man—a man worthier than he, a man without the baggage that rode on him like a backpack full of lead.

"What's going on?" Abby's words jerked him back to the reality of the moment, and he shook his head to clear the runaway thoughts.

Hannah offered Jude a half smile and stepped out the open front door. "You can do it." She only mouthed the words, but he easily caught them as Abby shuffled slowly toward the couch.

His lips twisted to the side, not really a smile, but the best he could do under the circumstances. Leave it to Hannah to be his cheerleader, his encourager, even when hours ago he was making a mental list of her negative traits. All of which now blurred and smeared around the edges, not really so negative after all.

The door clicked shut behind Hannah, and Abby slowly shuffled toward the couch. Toward him. Toward the truth. Jude's breath caught with anticipation and nerves. At least Hannah thought he was doing the right thing.

A fact which meant more than it should.

"Why did you leave the photo shoot earlier? Were you mad?" Abby crouched beside the loveseat, full of albums, and began turning pages. She frowned the faster she flipped. "Where did you get all these pictures of Mom?"

So many questions. Her innocence nearly broke Jude's heart. He took a deep breath, still not sure he was making the right decision. But it was too late now. He'd made a resolve on his way home from downtown a few hours ago, and there wasn't any going back. He couldn't keep going like this, dodging the truth, making excuses, protecting Abby from monsters she didn't understand. If he was ever going to have a chance at keeping her from turning out like her mom, he had to be honest.

Painfully honest.

"I've had them hidden away." Jude slowly sank into a chair, next to where Abby kneeled on the floor, and clasped his hands between his knees. "There are some things you don't know about your mom, and after today, I thought maybe you should."

"What do you mean?" Abby reached for the next album, the one that held Miranda's most recent pictures before she left. "She died when I was four. Right?"

"Yes, but that's not the whole story." Jude briefly squeezed his eyes shut. He'd never directly lied to Abby, but he let that assumption go on way too long. "Your mother was a professional model, Abby. You can see that from the pictures, I'm sure."

"Oh, wow. She was beautiful." Abby traced Miranda's face in a head shot, one that had been Jude's favorite at the time. Little did he know. "I have some pictures of her in my baby book, but I didn't know you had all these, too."

Jude wasn't sure why he kept them. Maybe because at first, he thought Miranda would come back. That she'd leave her preferred lifestyle of illegal substances and parties, and come back to her family. For a year or longer, he actually believed she would.

But then notice of her death had come through the front door, instead of Miranda herself, and the albums had sat collecting dust in a box in the attic for years until Jude almost managed to forget they were there.

Almost.

"Your mom made some bad choices, honey." Jude gently took the album from Abby's hands and closed it. "I didn't want you to know about them, but now I think it's time you do."

Abby's face paled and her eyes rounded.

He inhaled deeply. *God, I need Your help here. I know I don't deserve it, but Abby does. Please…* He released his breath with a huff. "Your mother left us, when you were little."

"What? Why?" Abby looked up at Jude from her perch on the floor, her expression stricken.

Here it was, the moment of truth. He kept his voice low and steady. "She wanted her career more than she wanted us. Or me, really." He might be confessing the truth, but he'd never let Abby think this was her fault. It wasn't. Miranda had loved her in own way, but it just hadn't been enough.

She'd loved the woman in the mirror more.

"What are you saying?" Abby's voice shrank,

tiny and vulnerable, and Jude reached toward her. But Abby moved away, her expression a question mark demanding an answer. "If she left us, then when did she die?"

Here it was. The moment of truth. Jude shook his head. "She overdosed on drugs one night in California, where she was working."

"No." Abby jumped up and shook her head, her hair falling across her face. She shoved it back, her gaze filling with tears. "She wouldn't do that."

Jude stood as well and stepped forward, gripping Abby's arms. "I know it's hard to hear but it's—"

Abby jerked away and Jude instinctively moved backward, away from the explosion. She planted her hands on her hips, her face angry but her voice full of grief. "I can't believe you."

The words spilled from Jude now, free of the dam that had stored them far too long. "I'm telling you the truth. Your mom wanted to pursue her modeling career, and she got mixed up in some bad things. Drugs and alcohol, and..." Well, he wouldn't say the rest. Jude ran his hand over his hair, wishing he'd practiced this before simply blurting out the facts. "It impaired her judgment. Her choices had nothing to do with you. Trust me, okay?"

Abby was quiet. Too quiet. He'd expected anger from her toward her mom. Grief. Maybe even denial at first. Once Jude had decided to make this confession, he'd braced himself for all of the potential emotions. She'd need to process, understandably, and he'd be ready to be her shoulder.

But he'd completely failed to prepare for what he saw lingering in his daughter's eyes.

Betrayal.

"Trust you? How can I?" Her words were barely a whisper, but they branded on his soul like a permanent stamp. "You lied to me."

Jude opened his mouth, but there was nothing more to say.

Without another word, Abby slipped down the hall to her room, the solid click of the door sounding like the final nail in a coffin.

Hannah flipped another page in her book, but she couldn't even remember the paragraph she'd just read. With a sigh, she shut the book and set it on her nightstand, then clicked off the lamp. She should be sleeping, but she couldn't stop wondering how Jude's talk with Abby had gone. She halfway hoped he'd call her that evening and share the details, but that was a little presumptuous.

Or maybe it meant it hadn't gone well and he was mad at Hannah for coaxing him to do it in the first place.

She adjusted her pillow under her neck and closed her eyes. Either way, at least the truth was out—that had to be for the best.

And either way, it didn't involve her.

Hannah's cell phone jangled, and she bolted upright, heart thundering. Who would be calling so late? It was already after 11:00 p.m. She grabbed the phone from her nightstand and yanked it free of the charger cord, then checked the caller ID, not recognizing the digits on the screen.

Her palms grew slick. "Hello?" Hannah pushed her hair out of her face, willing her heart to calm down. Probably a wrong number. No reason to panic.

"Ms. Hart?" A tiny voice sounded from the other end of the connection, followed by the rush of what sounded like traffic. A car horn blared, confirming her suspicions. "It's me. Abby."

"Abby?" Hannah pressed a hand over her chest, and drew a deep breath against the dread climbing up her throat. "Are you okay? Where are you?"

Another horn blared, and Abby's voice broke off due to the sketchy reception. "—out. Gas station on corner of...alone." She hiccuped a sob against another wave of static. "...got lost...scared."

Oh, no. Hannah scooted to the edge of the bed and grabbed a pen and paper from her top drawer. "Abby, tell me where you are again. Your phone is breaking up. Yell it if you have to."

That time, she got the cross streets Abby named, which were only a few miles from Hannah's house. She scribbled the address on the paper in case she forgot, then began throwing on a sweatshirt and shoes. "Don't go anywhere or talk to anyone. I'll be there in ten minutes." Seven if she pushed the speed limit.

Their connection broke off completely before Hannah could ask the obvious questions darting through her mind. She grabbed her purse and keys and jogged outside to her car, her mind racing faster than her legs. Why was Abby at a gas station alone? Where was Jude? And why hadn't she called her dad for help instead of her?

Apparently their talk hadn't gone well at all.

Exactly seven minutes later, Hannah slowed her SUV in front of the gas station Abby had mentioned, stomach tight with nerves. Though not far from where Hannah lived, this convenience store wasn't exactly in the best part of town. The parking lot proved deserted, a fact Hannah wasn't sure was a good sign or not. Being alone meant there weren't strangers bothering Abby, but there was also something to be said for safety in numbers.

She scanned the outside of the store for signs of Abby, but found none. Inside, a lone clerk slouched over her phone, oblivious to any customers. Where was Abby?

A flash of blond hair darted against the row of refrigerated drinks in the back of the store. Hannah honked the car horn. The head looked up, and Abby's eyes met hers over a row of Hostess desserts.

Nearly sick with relief, Hannah barely had time to unlock the doors before Abby was jumping in the car. She wrapped her arms around Hannah's neck and sobbed.

Hannah locked the doors back with her free hand, her other arm tight against Abby. "It's okay, you're safe. What happened?"

Abby pulled away, and for the first time, Hannah noticed her face was caked with makeup. Combined with the trendy clothes Abby had on and high heels, and she could pass for sixteen years old—especially to the wrong person. Dread filled Hannah's stomach.

"I snuck out." Abby sniffed, wiping her nose with the back of her hand, the motion smearing off a layer of foundation. Where had she even gotten all that stuff? Hannah dug in her console for a tissue, and handed it to Abby. She dabbed at her eyes, leaving a trail of mascara on each cheek. "I'm so sorry."

"Abby, why would you do that?"

A car door slammed behind Hannah, and two muscled, tattooed guys slowly approached the store. Time to go. She shoved the car into gear and gunned it out of the parking lot. "It's dangerous for you to be out alone. I know you think you're grown up, but sweetie, you're not."

"I know." Abby buckled her seat belt, then crossed her arms over her chest, shrinking into the seat. She suddenly looked a lot more like the young girl Hannah knew and loved.

Loved? She frowned, darting another glimpse at

Abby as she slouched in the passenger seat. Yes, loved. Regardless of what Jude felt—or didn't feel—for Hannah, she was officially attached to the girl. The maternal instincts that had roared to life tonight proved that much. She'd do anything to keep her safe, give her a sense of self-worth, of value.

Even if that meant being brutally honest.

Hannah stopped at a red light, double-checking that the doors were locked. "We're going to have to call your dad."

"No!" Abby shot upright in her seat, the belt straining against her chest. "Not yet. I want to talk to you first." She bit her lower lip, looking away. "I think you'll understand better."

"He needs to know you're safe." Hannah pulled out her cell. "Either you call him, or I will." She held out the phone.

The light turned green and Hannah drove an entire block before Abby finally took the cell and began to dial.

"Dad?" Abby's voice broke on the word, and Jude's voice boomed through the other end, loud and furious, though clearly tinged with relief.

Hannah's hands tightened on the wheel. *Come on, Jude, don't be angry.* Not first. Abby needed to know love first. Then discipline. If she was Abby's mom, that's how she'd handle it.

But she wasn't. The thought clocked her like a

fist to the stomach, and she swallowed hard as she made another turn toward their house.

Jude's voice immediately softened, as if he'd somehow heard her internal plea. Abby's face tightened with emotion as she explained who was taking her home, then she mumbled a short good-bye.

"He said to hurry." Abby slid Hannah's cell phone into the cupholder between them, and curled her legs up in the seat. She shivered. No wonder, with that short skirt she wore over sheer tights. Hannah cranked up the heater, then stopped at a stop sign and shifted in her seat to face Abby.

"Time for answers." She kept her tone firm, but welcoming. Hannah deserved answers, getting out of bed this time of night to rescue Abby. But more than that, Abby deserved the chance to share openly and freely with a woman she trusted.

And if Abby had put on *that* much makeup, it was definitely a woman-to-woman kind of issue.

"Dad and I had a fight." Abby adjusted the heater vent to blow toward her legs. "I found out he lied to me my entire life." The memory must have stirred up a fresh batch of anger, because the sorrow fled her expression, replaced by bitterness. "My mom didn't just die. She abandoned us. Me." She shook her head. "And she overdosed."

Hannah wasn't sure if she should admit she already knew that part, not wanting to hurt Abby further by implying that others knew before she did. But she couldn't lie. She kept her words neutral. "Maybe he just wanted to protect you."

"By keeping secrets?" Abby's voice rose in the confines of the car. "I don't think so." She wiped at her eyes again, and Hannah fished out a fresh tissue. "So I snuck out tonight. I didn't want to stay there with him. I was trying to go to my friend's house, but I got turned around in the dark." She groaned. "I can't believe I forgot a flashlight."

"What made you get scared? Being lost?"

"No. Well, sort of." Abby hesitated. "I stopped to try to look up her address on my phone. And while I was standing there, this guy drove by, and honked at me. Then drove back by, twice. I kept walking, but he followed me, yelling stuff out his window." Red heat colored Abby's cheeks, and she ducked her head, fiddling with the seam on her seat belt. "It was bad stuff."

"Oh, Abby." Hannah reached for her again, and held onto her hand. *God, give me the right words.* The prayer flowed naturally on Abby's behalf, much more naturally than when she'd attempted prayers for herself. She shook off that thought. "That was wrong of him. But do you know why he did that?"

She shrugged as if she didn't care, but her eyes pleaded to know.

"Because look at you." Hannah gestured to Abby's outfit: the see-through tights, the short skirt, the slightly revealing top. "I understand you aren't happy with your current wardrobe, but this outfit goes to the other extreme. It makes some boys—or men—think you're saying things you don't mean."

"I don't get it." Abby frowned, the innocence on her expression a stark contrast to the outfit hugging her body.

Poor Jude. Abby was at that time in her life where she needed a mom, not only for girl talk and positive influences, but because of all the delicate subjects coming up in her immediate future. She probably had learned a lot from school and from her friends, but some things needed to be discussed in person by a parent. It wasn't fair that Abby and Jude had to tread these waters alone. A wave of anger toward Abby's mom caught Hannah off guard, and she squelched it before it could run her off her goal. No wonder Jude struggled with his temper. She'd known Abby a matter of weeks, and already her instincts to protect her ran strong— strong enough to dislike someone she'd never even met.

"When you dress like this, you look a lot older than you are. So certain boys assume things." Hannah hesitated. "Bad things, like what that guy said to you."

"Oh." Abby averted her eyes, but understanding dawned in her features.

"You can be beautiful and still look good, and be trendy. But you don't need tons of makeup and short skirts to do it." Hannah tugged at Abby's skirt. "Where did you get this stuff, anyway?"

"Mya. It was all stuff her mom made her get rid of." She rolled her eyes. "Guess I see why now."

"And do you see that's why your dad feels the way he does about your appearance? He wants to keep you safe from the things that hurt your mom. From the things that took her off the right path and…" Hannah's voice trailed off and she swallowed before she could finish her sentence. "And killed her."

"So you already knew about her?" Abby squinted up at Hannah.

She slowly nodded. "Your dad has talked to me a little. And maybe his methods seem extreme sometimes, but you know he does it out of love. Protection and love go hand-in-hand."

"Yeah." Abby bit her bottom lip, turning to stare out the front window. "I guess I forgot that."

She appeared to be doing some heavy thinking, so Hannah remained silent and accelerated through the stop sign they'd been sitting at. As she began winding through neighborhood streets to Jude's house, she couldn't resist adding one more piece of truth to their talk.

"If you're ever unsure about what's appropriate to wear, you can ask me, okay? Tonight could have gone a lot differently, sweetie." It hurt her to stomach to think *how* differently, but she didn't need to put that kind of fear into Abby right now. Tonight's issues had been sufficient enough. *Thank You for protecting her, Lord.*

"Really? I can ask you?" They passed under a streetlight, and Hannah marveled at the hope lighting Abby's eyes. Was the poor girl that starved for a woman's confidence? No wonder she played endless matchmaker for her dad. Even if Abby hadn't realized it herself yet, she needed—craved—a mother figure in her life.

"Of course. Anytime." Hannah tapped the digital clock on the car's display, and grinned at Abby. "Though preferably before 9:00 p.m."

"Sorry." Abby grinned back, sheepish, looking more like the girl Hannah knew.

And loved.

They drove in silence for the remaining mile. As Hannah made the final turn onto Abby's street, the girl's soft voice pierced the quiet. "Ms. Hart?"

Hannah bumped over the curb and into the driveway. "Yes, sweetie?"

"I wish you were my mom instead."

The words washed over Hannah's heart, drowning it in a blanket of warmth and comfort—and regret.

Me, too.

Chapter Fifteen

The last time Jude's heart had beat this fast, he'd been trying out for the track team in high school. Not his forte, as evidenced by the stitch in his side and the blood pounding in his ears. But even that couldn't hold much of a comparison to nudging open Abby's door to tell her good-night and finding an empty bed.

He had stood in the middle of her room, staring at the haphazardly tossed covers, the open closet door, the makeup stains on her desktop, and couldn't breathe. Couldn't think.

A prayer had started on his lips, then tangled. *Grace. Mercy. God, please.*

Thankfully, his cell had rung about that same time, Abby's tear-streaked voice setting off even more alarms in his heart. She hadn't said where she was, only that Hannah was bringing her home and they'd be there in a few minutes.

Now he paced the living room, chest constricting as headlights flashed across the windows. Man, he wanted to yell. Lecture. Berate. By the time he was through, Abby would know better, that much was certain. She had to learn how dangerous her actions had been, how irresponsible, ungrateful…

The front door swung open and Abby rushed inside. She fell into Jude's arms, choking on her own sobs. "I'm so—so sorry." Her voice broke into a wail, carrying all traces of anger from Jude's body.

Jude hugged her back, clutching her head to his chest, feeling nothing but relief pouring for his soul. *Thank You, God.* "I know, honey." He smoothed Abby's hair, then looked up to see Hannah standing hesitantly in the open doorway. What was her role in this? Her face held remorse, and something else he couldn't quite define. And were those tears glistening in her eyes?

Jude gently pushed Abby away, long enough for her to wipe her own set of tears off her cheeks— that is, those that hadn't already dried into the makeup gooped on her face and racooned around her eyes. He took in the outfit she wore, her hunched shoulders and crossed arms proving she knew it wasn't right, and sighed. There'd be more to address later, but neither of them were up for it tonight. "Go to bed. We'll talk tomorrow."

Abby's eyes widened, and she swiped at a rogue tear that dripped toward her chin. "You're not mad?"

The shock in her voice cut like a knife, and guilt

flooded the recesses left by his anger. Maybe tonight's antics deserved a firm hand, but how many times in the past had Jude allowed stress and other factors to prematurely balloon his temper? Make him overreact?

He'd given his daughter reason over the years to expect the worst from him.

Jude's stomach clenched with regret. Yes, Abby needed discipline, and without question, she'd be punished for this latest stunt.

But tonight, she needed to know grace.

He tucked her hair behind her ear. "No, I'm not mad. Just glad you're safe."

"I'll never do it again." Abby's whisper cut through his heart, and he patted her back as he returned another tight hug.

"I'm keeping you to that." He pointed her toward her room, and Abby lifted one hand in goodbye to Hannah before slipping down the hall. Her door shut with a soft click.

Jude motioned for Hannah to step outside, and followed her onto the porch. The wooden boards were cold under his bare feet, yet the emotion welling inside heated him through and through. "I don't even know what to ask first." He hesitated. "But whatever you did, thank you. I know you weren't expecting to be up this late."

"I'm glad she trusted me enough to call. She could have really gotten into trouble." Hannah moved toward the porch swing, huddling into the oversize college sweatshirt she wore. She almost looked like she could be a college student herself, with her hair tucked back and her face devoid of makeup.

Jude sank down on the swing beside her, and set them moving with a push of his foot. "So what happened?"

Hannah explained about the late-night phone call, and what she found when she picked up Abby. "She was really mad at you. But also immediately sorry for what she'd done. She knew it was wrong the whole time." Hannah let out a sigh, and for the first time, Jude realized what stress Abby's decisions had put on her tonight, too. Hannah really cared—more than she had reason to. Was it possible Hannah had feelings that were beginning to match his own?

She continued, oblivious to the turmoil raging in Jude's stomach. "I think anger drove her out the door initially, but she wasn't running away. Just going to a friend's house."

"Did you get to talk to her about all that...stuff... she was wearing?" Jude hated the image of his daughter in such a get-up. It screamed Miranda, and made him want to cover his ears.

"Abby seems to understand that now, too. Especially after—" Hannah stopped suddenly and coughed, a stall if he'd ever seen one.

His eyes narrowed. "After what?"

"After what a guy said to her."

Jude's stomach seized, and his hands clenched into fists. He kept his jaw tight as Hannah filled in the blanks on the rest of Abby's late-night adventure. When she finally finished, he wasn't sure if he should thank God again for His grace—or slam his hand through the porch rail. The old Jude wanted to do the latter. But the Jude who was now brutally aware of his shortcomings knew he should go for the former.

Sadly, neither felt natural anymore.

"Are you okay?" Hannah angled her head toward him, eyes wide and luminous. Her hair shone in the moonlight streaming over his front yard, and suddenly, he didn't want to think about Abby. Or his temper. Or anything other than what it might be like to kiss Hannah.

"*Okay* might be stretching it." He leaned back and tilted his head toward her, their faces inches apart.

Hannah held his gaze for a long moment, long enough to give him hope she might actually allow a kiss, before she suddenly shifted, pushing the swing to gain momentum and turning her profile to Jude. She'd sat on his left side, so her profile appeared blemish free. On purpose? Probably.

He wished he could convince her that she didn't need to hide from him.

"I'm proud of you, you know." Hannah's voice broke the chorus of crickets chirping around them. "The way you handled Abby tonight—it couldn't have been easy. But it was exactly what she needed."

For once, confirmation of his parenting skills didn't offend Jude. Before, his instincts would have been to assume insult, to wonder what made Hannah think he or any other parent needed her approval. But tonight, he just felt grateful he had it.

Wanted more of it.

"Thank you." He stopped the swing with his foot, reaching up and brushing a strand of hair off Hannah's face. Her cheek was smoother than he'd imagined, and he gently coaxed her face toward him. "That means a lot."

Chemistry sizzled the air between them, his pulse racing now as he edged closer.

"Jude, don't." Hannah's hand came up, but instead of pushing him away, her fingers clenched his own in a lifeline, a complete contradiction to her words.

"Don't what?" He eased back enough to look her in the eye. "Pretend that you haven't gotten under my skin? Pretend like our lives haven't been better since you came along?" Jude's breath hitched in his chest, hope springing from somewhere deep within as Hannah's expression warmed. He trailed one finger down her scar toward her mouth, his eyes dropping to follow the motion. "Pretend like I haven't wanted to kiss you since the day I met you?"

Hannah's lips parted—all the invitation he

needed. Jude closed the distance between them, sealing her mouth with his own, wishing he could draw her closer but heeding the warning signals in his mind to go slowly. Hannah wasn't a woman to rush, no matter how desperately he felt otherwise. He braced himself for rejection, for Hannah to prove that holding her was much too good to be true.

But her hands reached up and slid along his neck, her fingers brushing the hair at the back of his collar and digging in deep. She returned his kiss with her own desperation and need. Had she ever truly felt wanted? What limitations had that scar put on her self-esteem? He'd willingly kiss Hannah all night if it would even begin to show her what an amazing woman she was, how much she had to offer.

How much he'd fallen for her.

If Hannah didn't know better, she'd have thought an earthquake shook Jude's yard. But it was only the reaction of her own heart, threatening to pummel out of her chest the longer she kissed Jude. She relished the safety of his embrace, the confidence of his gentle touch, the warm tingling in her spine that slid up her back. It was more than she'd ever imagined. It was perfect. It was...

A fairy tale.

Reality crashed upon Hannah like a bucket of cold water, and she jerked backward, breathless, covering her mouth with her hand. She couldn't do this, couldn't indulge Jude's momentary whim. He'd had a rough night, and she'd helped him. Of course he'd be thankful, and let emotions take over instead of logic. He didn't mean this—or at least wouldn't tomorrow. She was Hannah. He was Jude. They didn't agree about anything—especially concerning Abby. Not to mention her very profession reminded him of everything he wanted to forget, even boycott. It would never work. Opposites didn't always attract.

Sometimes they repelled.

"I'm sorry, I shouldn't have—"

Jude's apology stopped abruptly as Hannah threw one hand in the air to deflect it. "Don't. Don't apologize." That would make it worse, so much worse. At least tonight she could pretend he meant everything his kiss had said. Could embrace the fairy tale for a few more hours.

Jude's mouth clamped shut at the interruption, and Hannah couldn't help but revel in the way his lips had felt against her own. Had she ever been kissed like that? Even her fiancé had never put as much feeling into his affection. She quickly looked away, fighting for control, searching for resolve. Part of her wanted to dive right back into Jude's embrace.

But she knew it'd only hurt worse later.

"Hannah?"

His soft voice brought a well of tears to her eyes, and she blinked rapidly. "I'm fine."

Jude stiffened beside her. "You're crying."

"No, I'm not." He'd probably had more than enough tears tonight, between her and Abby. She widened her eyes to stop the prick of moisture and forced a smile. "See?"

"Nice save." Jude shifted back in the swing, giving her some space, and ran a hand over his hair. She'd never forget how his hair had felt in her fingers, smooth and soft without the gel that usually held it in place. Clad in jeans and a polo shirt that highlighted the muscle in his arms she didn't know he had, barefoot despite the chill of the autumn night. Relaxed. Comfortable.

He was much more dangerous without the suit.

"I didn't apologize because I regretted it." Jude smiled, slow and too charming for her own good. "Quite the contrary."

Her stomach fluttered, and she scooted an inch away, determined not to give in to the attraction. It was emotion, nothing more. Once Jude knew her secrets, he'd take off. Just like her fiancé. He and Abby deserved better. Someone who could be what they needed.

How she wished that could be her. If only Jude could be okay with her profession, could ease off his rules for Abby—could forget about wanting more kids one day. But he'd made his dreams clear enough in the weeks they'd known each other. Jude was destined to be a family man, deserved to have the big family he was robbed of. She couldn't be the reason he lost his dream—again.

She licked her lips, still tingling from his kiss, and struggled to think of a response to his comment that wouldn't dig the hole she'd started deeper.

His husky voice murmured, low in her ear as his arm slid around her shoulders. "Why are you running?"

Hannah's gaze collided with Jude's, his eyes full of confusion and compassion, like maybe he already knew. No, that was impossible. She fought the urge to snuggle into his embrace, keeping her back stiff instead. But his warmth beckoned, and she found herself relaxing against him, despite her best intentions. "I'm not running."

"Jogging, then."

She choked back a laugh, grateful for his lighter tone.

"I'm serious, Hannah. If it's your scar, you know I don't care." Jude's finger traced the line on her cheek once again, and despite knowing better, she closed her eyes, leaning into his touch. Maybe he didn't care now. But he would later. Everyone did later.

"It's complicated." She opened her eyes and pulled away, averting her gaze. But not fast enough to see the hurt flicker across his expression.

The wind stirred, cutting through Hannah's

shirt, making her miss Jude's warmth even more than she already did. She hunched inside her sweatshirt, wishing she could drape the entire thing over her head and hide.

He leveled his gaze at her, shifting in the swing to face her completely. "I've done complicated before."

"And you deserve better." Her whispered words barely carried over the rustling of the tree limbs. Better than her, to be sure. At least now she knew he wasn't still pining for his ex-wife. But that didn't clear any of the obstacles before her. If anything, knowing his heart was open to Hannah made the obstacles more daunting.

He frowned at her. "I don't know what you see when you look in a mirror, but I have a hunch it's about a two-inch area only."

"Three."

"It gives you character, you know. Tell me what happened."

The coaxing command broke through her defenses, and Hannah drew a deep breath. He'd earned an explanation, especially after the way he'd willingly blurted his secrets to her. "It was a car wreck. About two years ago." She looked down at her scuffed sneakers. "It was pretty bad." To put it mildly.

"If you walked away with just a scar, Hannah— that's a miracle." Relief tinged Jude's voice, and she didn't have the heart to correct him. "I know I'm not an expert, but I'd imagine that means God still has big plans for you."

"I know." She believed that much. Except that now, His plans didn't match up with her own. Maybe that was the source of the real problem—not so much feeling abandoned in her personal storm, but rather losing control of her life. All she ever wanted had been a husband, children and a successful career.

Settling for one out of three burned worse than her injury had.

Hannah loved photography, but not enough to have it alone define the rest of her days. But what options did she have now? Not many. She wasn't getting any younger. It seemed all the good men were claimed, or weren't interested in damaged goods.

She didn't really blame them.

"Give me a chance, Hannah." Jude's eyes pleaded with hers, soft and understanding. If only he knew the full truth, if only he could tell her that it wouldn't matter, that he didn't care if he had a big family one day, didn't mind not having a bloodline to carry on the family name. *Oh, God, this really isn't fair.* She wanted to give in, to cave to his gentle encouragement. But to what end?

He reached over and cupped her cheek with his hand, his thumb trailing her scar once again. "One chance. Let me show you how I see you."

Of all the romance novels Hannah had ever read,

she'd never dreamed a line as good as that one. And looking into Jude's eyes, she knew it wasn't a line. He meant it, heart and soul.

He just didn't have all the information.

"We're too different." The excuse sounded thin, even though it was truth. She pressed on. "You can't stand what I do for a living. How can we make anything work if you shudder every time I take a picture?"

"What if I worked on that?" The resolve in Jude's voice sent tremors down Hannah's back. Would he really do that for her? Put aside his prejudices and biases and lifetime of pain—for her?

Something snapped inside Hannah then, begging for release, longing to be free of the bondage of the past. She wanted a breath of the future.

But she could only inhale the past.

"I just can't." She eased away from his touch on her cheek, instantly missing his warmth and the assurance of his embrace. But she was doing him a favor. She had to remember that.

"Okay." Jude didn't back away, but neither did he press toward her. He remained solid on the swing next to her, a spark of determination in his eyes. "But I'm going to change your mind. You'll see."

Oh, how she wished he could.

Chapter Sixteen

Hannah couldn't believe she'd agreed to this—
and even more than that, couldn't believe Jude had
offered.

"A nature walk? Really?" she'd said in the parking lot of church the next morning, when he'd first
brought up the idea. She'd tagged along to the service again at Abby's insistence, intending to meet
Sophia for brunch after.

He'd only grinned at her surprise. "It'll be fun.
Hey, you said you'd help show me a different side
of photography." He'd shrugged. "What better
place than in the great outdoors?"

"I'm not exactly a big outdoors kind of girl." Her
protest had been weak, and Jude knew it. Abby's
insistence—and Hannah's vulnerability toward her
after walking with her through last night's storm—
had sealed the deal, and the next thing Hannah
knew, she'd agreed to pack a picnic lunch and meet
them at the park trails at one o'clock.

Now, two hours later, as her thighs burned with
the effort of hiking and her camera strap rubbed a
raw spot on her neck, Hannah wondered what she'd
gotten into. Was Jude really interested in changing his mindset toward photography? Or was this
a ploy to "change *her* mind," as he'd mentioned on
the porch?

The memory of his kiss danced through Hannah's thoughts, releasing a flock of butterflies in
her stomach that she mentally captured and locked
away. Jude might be willing to make a relationship
with her work, but she knew better. He was different from her ex-fiancé in many ways, but Jude was
still a man—one who wanted a kids and a family
bloodline to pass down to the next generation.

They weren't really so different after all.

Hannah forced the unpleasant thoughts away and
increased her pace to catch up with Jude, leaves
crunching under her feet. It was too pretty an afternoon to get bogged down with reality. She'd spent
more than enough time fretting over the past. She
wasn't about to start feeding dismal thoughts of the
future, too. For once, she'd enjoy today, and it'd be
enough.

It had to be.

Abby pranced ahead, stopping every few minutes to examine a particularly interesting leaf, or
squeal over a spider web. Hannah's lungs huffed
in effort to process the cool air streaming over the
hilltops, and she paused to catch her breath.

"It's so refreshing out here." Jude stopped and gestured to the woods, crimson and burnt orange in all their autumn glory. With his backpack of picnic supplies, long-sleeved T-shirt and track pants, he looked like he hiked every day. "I can feel the stress from work easing away." He chuckled. "Of course, I'm sure it'll be back. But this is nice."

"It really is, though my lungs might not agree." Hannah drew another deep breath, grateful the pinch in her side had started to ease, and gestured to Abby. "Seems like she's doing good after last night's misadventure."

"We had a big talk during breakfast today, before church." Jude moved a low-hanging branch out of their way as they resumed their pace. "I think we're in a much better place."

"I'm glad." Abby's late night escapade had definitely been dangerous, but maybe it had worked out for the best, drawing her and her dad to an understanding they hadn't had before. As the pastor said in his sermon that very morning, God was able to work all things for good. Romans chapter eight said as much.

Hannah touched her cheek. It'd be nice to believe that truth for herself, but so far, the evidence wasn't there. *I want to believe, God. Show me how.* Somehow, out here on the trail, her prayer seemed to be heard by the Almighty. Or was that because she was making an effort again, going to church, putting herself in a place to be heard? Not that God only resided in church, but in the chaos and busyness of life it was much easier to shut Him out than in a pew, surrounded by fellow congregation members searching for answers.

Searching for Him.

"Hey, Dad, Ms. Hart. Look at this!" Abby called to them from down the trail. They hurried to catch up to her, and Abby pointed to the tree trunk of a nearby pine. "Isn't it cool?"

Hannah gently touched the bark, where a couple had carved their initials and a heart into the wood. "This would be a great shot." She took the lens cap off her camera and snapped from several different angles. The afternoon sun cutting through the leaves provided the perfect lighting.

"But you don't even know who these people are." Jude touched the letters. B.M, and J.R.

"That's the beauty of it. The mystery." Hannah traced the letters for herself. "Imagining who they are, when they did this. If they're still together." She looked up, finally realizing she'd been staring at the trunk. "You know?"

"Maybe." Jude shrugged, but he didn't look convinced. But then again, he was a principal—disciplined, organized, methodical. Totally left-brained.

She smiled. "Just wait. When I get them developed, you'll see what I mean."

"I'll take your word for it."

He offered a return smile, and Hannah wished she could capture that particular form of beauty on film, too. But no taking pictures of people. That was the rule she'd made for herself today. As much as she wanted to snap photo after photo of Abby in this rural, woodsy backdrop, she restrained. Baby steps, for Jude's sake—and honestly, for hers, too.

Because with every click of the shutter, Hannah found herself wishing these family outings could one day become exactly that.

"I bet this couple wrote this when they teenagers, and now they're old and bald and have fifteen grandkids." Abby twirled in a circle beside Hannah, grinning, all traces of rebellious teen gone.

"Fifteen grandkids, huh? That's all?" Jude plucked a handful of leaves from a nearby tree and tossed them at Abby.

"Hey! You got them in my hair. And I think big families are cool." She bent over and scooped up an armload, returning the attack.

He let loose with a second round of leaves. "I agree." Jude winked at Hannah, and her heart faltered. If only...

Romans 8, God? Can you prove that one?

With a shriek, Abby ducked behind the carved pine. "That's it. You're going down, Dad."

Hannah stepped aside, out of the line of fire as they each gathered their next round of leaves, and discreetly took pictures of the dueling father-daughter duo.

Maybe some rules were meant to be broken.

* * *

Jude's office felt downright stifling after spending yesterday in the woods. Already he missed the clean scent of pine needles, the scuffle of golden leaves under his feet and those amazing sandwiches Hannah had thrown together after church for their picnic. Though to be honest, he'd have been fine with one of those prepackaged, processed meat and cheese trays that Abby devoured as a child as long as he was with Hannah.

He'd already changed his computer screen background to a default scene of the woods, just because it reminded him of her and the fun they'd had yesterday. To say he had it bad for Hannah felt a little like a lie, or at best, an extreme understatement. As soon as he'd given his heart freedom to pursue her, it'd anxiously jumped right on the idea, surprising even himself with the intensity of his feelings.

There were still obstacles, of course. He'd tried to pretend he hadn't noticed her taking shots of him and Abby during their scuffle with the leaves, tried to pretend he didn't care—but he did. He didn't want it to bother him anymore, but old habits lingered. However, if anyone could break down the defenses he had in that department, it'd be Hannah.

He couldn't wait to let her keep trying.

Jude rolled a pen between his fingers as he studied the golden leaves on his computer screen. Of course, there was also the slight obstacle of convincing Hannah to give him—them—a chance.

At least he had Abby on his side. It seemed she wanted him to win Hannah's heart as much as he wanted to. Abby had been eager regarding all of her matchmaking attempts in the past, but with Hannah, it was different. Maybe because Hannah had invested in her before Abby even tried to fling heart-shaped arrows.

He kicked his feet up and leaned back in his chair, content to stare at the computer and remember yesterday. He'd made progress with Hannah, he could tell. She felt the same way about him, it was obvious in her eyes. He just needed to figure out how to break down the barrier she kept hiding behind. Was it simply the insecurities related to her scar? Or something else he didn't know about?

"Bradley?" Principal's Coleman's gruff voice startled Jude, and he slipped sideways in his chair as he struggled to right himself. His feet landed on the floor with a thud.

"Sir." Breathless, Jude sat up straight, trying to compose himself and fighting the blush at being caught relaxing during the workday. He'd never been one to lounge around and procrastinate— much less daydream—but then again, he'd never had a five-four, dark-eyed, silky-haired reason to do so.

"I'm actually glad to see you're not in here stressing out over the budget." Coleman didn't sit, but rather stood in front of Jude's desk. A hint of a smile shaded his eyes, which seemed as weary as Jude had felt last week—before Hannah. Before their kiss. Before he realized there was a lot more to life than arguments with his daughter and keeping secrets and slowly becoming a workaholic.

Jude smiled, careful to keep it toned back to half the level he actually felt inside. No sense in scaring off his superior. "So am I."

Coleman continued. "I'm assuming that means you must have already completed the proposal."

With a swift click, Jude closed out the mostly blank document on his computer—the one that should be filled with his carefully prepared research and stats for pitching to the school board. "I wouldn't say completed."

Coleman's eyebrows bunched together, but he didn't comment. Instead, he rocked back on his heels and jingled the change in his pocket as he always did while mulling something over.

Jude didn't want him to mull too long. "Of course it will be done in time for the meeting Wednesday." He straightened his shoulders, trying to project confidence. "I've had a little trouble narrowing down the options." If you could call choosing between his best friend's job and his daughter's favorite hobby *options*. Not to mention Hannah was now a factor, as she clearly took Abby and Sophia's side in the art versus sports debacle. There would be no way to keep everyone happy—

especially the parents, faculty and community as a whole. Everyone had an opinion, and none of them would match up.

"The meeting has actually been postponed a few days. That's what I came in here to tell you." Coleman smiled, though it didn't seem to reach his eyes. Jude swallowed. He knew of Jude's lack of progress, judging by that smirk. Easy for him— he'd chosen not to have to carry the weight of the school for this one, but rather passed it on. "I'll need your proposal ready to present on Monday evening."

That gave him an extra five days. Less than one week to figure out the impossible. Better than nothing, but in a way, he'd been ready to get the entire thing over with. Jude adjusted his tie, eager to do something with his hands before he started twiddling his thumbs. "It'll be done, sir." Somehow.

"Do you know how you're going to pitch it yet?" Not a clue. He cleared his throat. "I'd prefer completing my research and gathering my data before saying." True, though there wasn't much to tell yet. Again with the understatements. His thoughts flicked to Hannah, then back. No use going there right now—or even after his boss left. He could plan his next attempt at winning Hannah later this evening, when he wasn't staring a blank computer document that refused to type itself. First things first.

Though somehow, Hannah kept sneaking into that role.

Coleman leaned forward, bracing his hands on Jude's desk and breaking into his reverie. A whiff of peppermint and cigarette smoke drifted toward Jude. "May I offer you some encouragement, off the record?"

Jude nodded, fighting the urge to cough. "Of course." Anything to help him move forward, feel less guilty about the choice he'd have to make, one way or the other. The school board might not choose what he presented, but his instincts told him that everyone in this game wanted to point fingers at someone else. And he was the easiest target. If he pitched a smart idea, they'd likely go for it if only for the sole reason of wanting to keep their hands clean. Maybe Coleman had a solution that would help ease the burden after all.

He lowered his voice. "Ditch the art department, and save the sports."

"Sir?" Jude's eyebrows hiked up his forehead. "It's not that easy. There's a lot of different factors to con—"

"It's strictly my opinion." Coleman's hands slid off the edge of the desk as he righted himself and headed for the door. "You do what you think best."

Yet the tone in his voice indicated the exact opposite. If Coleman already knew what was best, why didn't he just specifically tell Jude what to prepare? Then Jude's own thoughts came back to him, clearer than before. Because of getting to point fingers. It was a lot easier to throw Jude under the bus, especially to the media once the decision became official, than take the heat himself as head of the school.

The door clicked shut behind Coleman as he exited, and Jude reluctantly pulled the document back up, staring at the blinking cursor as pros and cons danced before his eyes.

What did he do? Save the sports department, his best friend's job, and keep the majority of the school and community—and his boss—happy? Or did he save his daughter's favorite hobby, the one outlet she'd had to keep her stable throughout the past two years of turmoil in their home? There was also the fact that losing the art department would put Sophia out of work and Jude considered her one of the top teachers in the school. Not to mention Hannah's best friend.

His head hurt.

Jude finally put his fingers to work, getting his chaotic thoughts onto the screen, and organized his pro/con list into columns by department. After several minutes, he maximized the screen and leaned back to view what'd he configured.

The answer was painfully clear.

Chapter Seventeen

Wednesday afternoon, Hannah peered over Sophia's shoulder at the finished magazine and couldn't help the burst of pride rising in her chest. "It really looks good. I still can't believe we got it ready so fast." The kids had done a fantastic job—both in the actual work, and in their dedication and motivation to see the project through. Hannah had never been prouder of them.

"No kidding. Here it is, not even a week after we took all the pictures—though I guess you pressing the kids to finish their written articles over the weekend helped move things along." Sophia flipped another page in the magazine, and laughed at the photo of Peter throwing the donuts at the girls.

Hannah smoothed one hand over the open booklet. It wasn't fancy. They'd printed it on regular paper rather than glossy, so it actually resembled more of a colored newspaper than anything else.

They'd also had to painstakingly staple each and every one of the three hundred copies, choosing to do so rather than pony up the money to take it to a professional printer. But the pictures had come out well, not grainy as Hannah had first feared as she sat with Lana during the first printing on Monday afternoon, and the overall effect felt as it should—fun, informative and sincere. Hopefully people would not only buy it and contribute to the cause, but also attend the many fundraisers they'd scheduled over the next few months.

"I guess now we wait and see what happens." Sophia shut the magazine and tossed it on the table in the electives classroom. "After distribution, of course." The students would be there for CREATE any minute. After getting permission from all the parents, Sophia planned to take them around the neighborhoods within walking distance of the school and distribute the magazines door-to-door, and wherever else they ran into people out and about willing to shell out ten dollars per issue. They'd marked the magazine higher than they'd originally intended, hoping the effort would show consumers how important the magazine was to the kids. Though Sophia had already confessed she'd allow customers to bargain down if need be—any cash would be better than none.

Though Hannah couldn't imagine anyone looking into the eager faces of the teens and turning them down.

"While you're walking the block with the kids, I'll take my car and talk to the folks at the bakery downtown." Hannah picked up several copies from the pile on the table and tapped them neatly together. "They'd probably like some to sell for us, since we posed in front of their awning."

"Good idea. And maybe the thrift store and the bookstore would put some up, too." Sophia began fanning herself with a magazine copy, despite the cool temperature inside the school. "We'll need all the publicity we can get."

"Everyone will be on our side. No one wants to see an elective cut." Hannah perched on the edge of the work table and fanned her friend with a second magazine. "I saw the announcement about the big meeting on the news last night. Are you nervous?"

Sophia huffed. "Are you kidding? I get hot flashes every time I realize that in a few days, my career could end."

"Not technically. Remember, the budget doesn't take effect until next semester."

"So I'd be let go at the holidays. Perfect."

"I really don't think you need to worry." Hannah rolled in her lower lip but couldn't contain her smile. She believed in Jude and the decision he'd make. Surely he'd seen the goodness that CREATE brought to Abby, the passion that lit her eyes when she talked about saving her club.

And talk she did. Despite her reservations, Hannah, Abby and Jude had spent every evening together since their Sunday afternoon hike—eating out, grilling in Jude's backyard and laughing with Abby over the silly stories she told about her day. It'd been amazing to witness the change in Jude and Abby's relationship. Jude no longer flinched every time Abby mentioned the magazine fundraiser or the photos she'd been in, and he even let her wear jeans and a trendy top when they went out to Mario's one night. He'd really been trying to change. The leash he'd kept Abby on for so many years was slowly lengthening, and Abby was handling her tentative freedom with a healthy helping of responsibility.

Hannah shook her head at the memories. She was bonding with the father-daughter duo more than she ever thought possible—and quickly. Too quickly. Yet it'd been hard to convince her heart to slow down and not get involved when everything about her wanted to dive into their family and call it her own. The fears that consumed her just days ago now felt a little fuzzy, a little less clear. She debated telling Jude the truth, just getting the facts out there and seeing what happened. Maybe he could be different than her fiancé. Maybe he could prove her wrong.

But did she have the courage to try?

He already was different in so many ways. He talked with Hannah, really communicated in a way she never had with a man. Monday night after Abby had gone to her room to do homework, Jude had seemed distracted. Instead of brushing off his worries, he'd admitted his stress over the upcoming public proposal meeting. And no wonder—word among the teachers was that the sports department would stay and the arts would go. It had to be rough going into the meeting knowing Jude would be stating otherwise. There'd be backlash to deal with, for certain.

Hannah cleared her throat. "Jude will do the right thing. I believe in him. Maybe we'll be turning all this fundraiser money over to the sports department to try to save them, instead."

"I don't have that same confidence." Sophia fanned herself faster, the flapping of the booklet loud in the deserted classroom. "But then again, I'm not the one getting cozy with Jude on a regular basis."

"Sophia!" Hannah lightly popped her friend on the arm with her rolled up magazine and bit back an embarrassed laugh. "I'm not getting cozy with him. I'm hanging out with Abby."

"And Jude."

"Well, of course he's there." The burn in her cheeks made her denial pointless, and Sophia knew it.

Her friend smiled, but the humor didn't seem to make it to Sophia's eyes. "I'm happy for you, Hannah. Really. You know I've been pestering you for years to get a life again." She sighed. "I just don't think your new…friendship…with Jude will affect his business decisions."

"It *is* just a friendship. You don't have to make air quotes when you say that." Hannah crossed her arms over her sweater, her heart tapping an incessant rhythm beneath. "And I'm not saying I've convinced him of anything, but rather the facts have. The art department has tried too hard and is too good of a program to eliminate. Jude sees that."

Sophia lips twisted to the side in silent disagreement.

"Just wait. You'll see. The art department will be taken off the chopping block, and all this fundraiser money will either go to the sports department or be used for special projects for CREATE. Whatever they want." Hannah offered an encouraging smile. "There will be options."

The scuffle of feet and the chimes of laughter from the hallway signaled the arrival of the CREATE club. "You're right. We'll see." Sophia dropped her magazine on the table and grabbed two giant tote bags from under the desk. "I just hope we're seeing the same thing."

"Have some faith," Hannah whispered as she helped stuff the copies into the first bag. She smiled at the students as they crowded excitedly around the table, flipping through the magazine and exclaiming again over each aspect as if they'd never seen it. She nodded toward them. "They do."

Sophia studied the youths with a wary expression. "They don't know enough to think differently. They came up with this great idea, made it happen and are fully expecting it to work. Whereas you and I know that if Jude doesn't save the art department, then the little bit of money we raise from this effort will at best delay the inevitable—if nothing at all."

"When did you get so negative about this whole thing?" Hannah slid the last magazine into a second tote and stood it upright on the desk. Sophia was right about the money—no way would the magazine, even at ten dollars each, come close to meeting the budget needs of the department. But that hadn't been the goal—they were raising awareness more than anything else, which was most important at the moment. The money could come later, if people knew to give. And any cash they did raise could only benefit either department.

Sophia plucked a loose string off one of the tie-dye printed bags. "I have to admit, Hannah, I never thought from the beginning this fundraiser was more than just a fun way to help the kids feel like they did all they could. A way for them to be able to look back with no regrets and know they did their best."

"Jude would never suggest the board choose the sports department over the art department now, not when the kids showed all this heart." Hannah picked the smaller bag up and shouldered the straps. "They're the only ones trying. That'll count for something." Not to mention the way his relationship with Abby had progressed. No way would Jude endanger her favorite club and risk the tentative truce with his daughter. Business was business, but family was family.

Sophia's lips pursed. "Again, I'm not so sure. I know how the school system works, Hannah. It's not always pretty, or fair."

Hannah briefly closed her eyes. If she were in Sophia's position—stressed over possibly losing her job, overworked, underpaid and grossly underappreciated—she'd let the negativity get the best of her, too. After all, how many times had she been a Debby Downer in the days after her car accident?

A blush warmed Hannah's cheeks. Or even more recently than that.

She patted Sophia's shoulder. "I'm here for you regardless of what happens. But I really feel good about it. Just trust, okay?"

"Who? The school board? Jude? Principal Coleman?" Sophia snorted. "I respect them all, but I'm not putting my hopes in any of them."

"Then trust God."

Sophia hiked an eyebrow at Hannah as she shouldered her bag. "You first."

Hannah strolled toward the teachers' lounge to get a drink before delivering the magazines, replaying her words to Sophia over and over in her head. Three simple little words, yet they'd flown off her lips before she could censor them.

Though for the first time in two years, Hannah didn't think she wanted to. It felt right, talking about God again, believing that Someone was taking care of her and the things she cared about. She'd missed that confidence, that security. She missed her faith.

But that didn't mean she had to open her heart up to Jude to prove it. Didn't have to put herself in a position to be broken again. Couldn't she have her faith back without having to test it so quickly?

Guilt pressed against Hannah's stomach as she pulled open the door to the teachers' lounge. No wonder she seemed like a hypocrite to Sophia. She apparently still had some things to work out for herself before she could preach to her friend. Maybe once Jude made his announcement Monday, Sophia would relax and give God more than just one Sunday to offer His peace and provision. Maybe then she'd believe the change Hannah was beginning to glimpse.

Maybe then Hannah would be ready to fully embrace it herself.

Lost in her thoughts, Hannah headed for the drink machine, counting the change in her hand and nearly ran into a tall figure. "Sorry!" She dodged back and looked up to see Russell, Jude's friend and basketball coach.

He looked up from the book he'd been flipping

through and grinned. "My fault. I shouldn't be loitering by the vending machines."

"Hey, it's not called the teachers' lounge for nothing." Hannah slid her coins into the dispenser, her bag full of magazines bumping her hip. "I was daydreaming."

"I'd ask what about, but I think I already know."

Another blush worked its way up Hannah's neck, warming her cheeks. "I'm not— Jude and I aren't—"

"My bad. I won't embarrass you anymore." Russell laughed as he tossed his book onto the table and pulled change from his pocket. "I spend too much time with my team. It's a guy thing, harassing each other."

"It's all right." At least Russell considered her a part of the school enough to tease her. It felt good to belong—even if her time at Pecan Grove Junior High was almost up.

Hannah plucked her soda from the opening in the machine and stepped back so Russell could choose his drink. As she popped the tab on the can, her eye caught the publication Russell had been reading. "Hey, that's our fundraiser magazine. What do you think?" She patted her bagful of copies.

"It's great. Very professional, considering what they had to work with." Russell punched the button for a cherry soda and waited while the can rumbled out. "I think the students did an excellent job."

"They certainly worked hard." Hannah took a sip of her drink, the carbonation tickling her throat. "I guess we'll know soon that it was all worth it."

Russell thumped the top of his can before cracking it open. "Yeah, I hope those fundraisers they cooked up raise enough money to help the art department stick around, too. At least for a while longer."

Hannah frowned. "What do you mean, awhile longer?" She hesitated. "Don't you know Jude's proposal plans?" Surely he would have told Russell, his best friend, his plans to save the art department. Though come to think of it, Jude had never actually spoken those words to her, either. She'd assumed.

Her heart broke into a spastic rhythm. No. Surely not.

"I do. Don't you?" Russell quirked an eyebrow. "I mean, I just assumed he'd have told you. Since you're...whatever you are... Wait. I guess you just said you *aren't*—"

Hannah waved her hand, cutting off the questions she couldn't easily answer, either. "I don't understand." She shifted her drink to her other hand, her fingers cold. She clenched them into a fist. "Are you saying Jude is planning a pitch to save the sports teams?"

"Of course. Why would you expect otherwise?" Russell's eyes darted to the magazine on the table, and then back to Hannah. Understanding dawned. "Oh. I see."

Hannah's jaw set and she shuffled her feet, her entire body suddenly heavy. "I think I do, too."

There. It was done.

Jude leaned back, eyes bleary, and studied the document on his computer that he really should read one more time but couldn't muster the energy to do so—much less the desire. He didn't really like what the black text read, even though he'd been the one to write it. But what choice did he truly have? Principal Coleman had made it seem like he had the decisions to make, all the choices, but his last visit to Jude's office Monday hinted at the opposite. As did the letters to the editor he'd read in the Tuesday morning newspaper and the hundred emails crowding the school's inbox, some bearing subject titles too hateful to even open. Jude's hands were tied.

But he had a sinking feeling there were two females in his life who weren't going to view it that way.

A sharp rap sounded on his partially open door. Jude glanced up to see Hannah framed in the doorway, eyes wide. She held a soda can in one hand, her face flushed almost as red as the aluminum, the scar she worked so hard to hide an angry white slash on her cheek in comparison.

"Hannah! What's wrong?" He stood, nearly

knocking over the desk chair. "Is it Abby? I thought she was going out with CREATE today to deliver those magazines." His heart beat an unsteady rhythm as adrenaline poured through his veins.

Hannah advanced slowly into his office, her movements overly tight and controlled, and set a full bag on top of his desk. "The pointless magazines, you mean. You've already made your decision, haven't you?"

Oh. Now Jude recognized the heat in her face for what it was—anger, not fear. He slowly sank back into his chair, too exhausted to stand and fight. "Sit down, please." He gestured to the seat across from him, his hand still shaky from the unnecessary adrenaline rush.

"No thanks. I prefer to stand." Hannah set her drink on his desk and crossed her arms, chin lifted. She was the spitting image of the fiery woman who stormed into his office a week ago, one with a mission and license to kill. She had "mama bear" written all over her face, and Jude didn't need a master's degree to know what was coming next. "I just heard a rumor that I'm starting to believe is actually the truth."

"And which one is that?" Jude raked his hand over his face and leaned back, wanting her to say it, to accuse him out loud. He'd been sitting in this office all week pouring over data and preparing a proposal that sat like a lead weight in his gut, and had zero choices about. Not if he wanted to please his boss and the entire community at large. Artsy women like Hannah and Sophia didn't understand—they were a minority. Parents in Pecan Grove wanted to stand on the sidelines and chug Gatorade and cheer for their sons on the field, wanted to see scholarship requests in the mail—not praise a portrait well painted or a picture well taken.

Hannah took a step closer, his desk pressing against her jean-clad legs as she leaned forward and braced her hands on the top. "The proposal." She jerked her head toward his monitor, where the truth lay bare. "You're axing the art department."

"*I'm* not doing anything." Jude fought the urge to lean forward, nose to nose, and show her he wasn't used to be bullied. But if he got that close, he'd kiss her again, and at the moment, such a move would likely earn him a black eye. "The board has the final say."

"But you've said yourself this entire time that your influence matters. That's why you're preparing the proposal in the first place." Hannah shook her head, her hair swinging across he shoulders. "How could you do this to the art students? They worked so hard on this fundraiser." She narrowed her eyes. "How could you do this to Abby?"

He knew she'd play that card, but he still felt the zing straight into his heart. "This isn't about Abby. This is business. I'm doing what the community wants—what my boss wants." Jude tapped his computer screen with one finger. "I don't have a choice."

Maybe a small part of Jude felt a little relieved at the notion. Abby might see it as his fault at first, but eventually she'd get over it and realize he'd done what had been expected of him by his superiors. And in the meantime, Jude could relax knowing that over the next year, she'd be free of the artistic influences that had caused so many fights between them this semester. It really would be for her greater good.

All while Sophia hit the road with nothing but a letter of reference and those ridiculous oversize bags she always carried around.

His stomach clenched.

"You don't believe any of that that. I can see it in your eyes." Anger faded from Hannah's expression, replaced with a steady sheen of disappointment. "You always have a choice."

"Hannah, I wish it was that simple."

"Who cares if it's complicated? The right thing isn't always easy." Hannah rocked back on her heels, face taut. "But it's always worth it."

"Who's to say saving the art department is even the right thing, anyway?" Jude stood, the desk still between them, and leaned forward, mimicking her earlier position. "It's your opinion. And Abby's, and maybe ten other people's. But I can assure you it's not the majority opinion."

She refused to back down, which was both frustrating and at the same time, admirable. "So maintaining your new relationship with your daughter isn't the right thing?" Her voice broke and she brushed at her face, but not before Jude saw the tears glistening in her eyes.

He drew a deep breath as he tried to see things from her side. He guessed this would look like a personal slam after the efforts he'd made toward her the past week. But surely she could see, this was for the best. The numbers didn't lie. "Hannah, I've been working hard on this project, and stressing to the point of nearly getting an ulcer. You have to trust me, that this is the right thing for the school and for the students."

"And the right thing for Abby?"

His mouth opened, then closed, and a disappointed victory lit Hannah's eyes as he proved her point. "My hands are tied."

"I guess this was inevitable. I wanted to trust you but…" She backed away toward the door, even as a tear escaped and slid down her cheek.

"What are you saying? That you'll let this come between us? I thought we were making progress. Do you really want to lose that? Because of this?" Jude nodded toward the proposal, wishing now he could dump the computer in the trash can and walk away from the entire thing. But he couldn't. This was his career, his source of income and provision for his family. He had to see it through and meet the challenge head-on, like always.

He just couldn't bear it if Hannah was a casualty in the process.

"It's not just this, Jude. I tried to tell you from the beginning—this was inevitable. Impossible." She hiccuped back a tiny sob as she gestured between the two of them, sounding so vulnerable it made him want to hold her and beg her to understand his position.

But pushing wouldn't help. He'd done that before with a woman, and it'd earned him a death certificate.

Jude steadied himself against his desk before speaking. "I know you're angry right now, and hurt, but there's no reason to say that. Nothing is impossible."

"I'm afraid I have to disagree." Hannah laughed, the sound filled with more annoyance than humor.

"What was it we just heard in church, Hannah? About nothing being impossible with God. About God working all things for good for those who—"

"I can't have children."

Jude stumbled forward, his eyes colliding with hers as fresh tears filled the void left from those streaking down her face. "What?" Surely he misunderstood. Hannah was young and healthy and—

"The car wreck." Her hand went to the scar on her cheek. "I can't have kids."

Shock mingled with confusion coursed through

Jude's veins, leaving him light-headed. He fumbled for a grip on the edge of the desk and missed, sitting down hard in his chair. "But how— What—"

"I had an emergency hysterectomy because of my injuries." Hannah covered her face with both hands, then trailed her fingers down to her chin with a shudder. "There. Now you know."

Jude couldn't believe it. No wonder that scar beat her up so mercilessly every day. Reality slammed his gut like a sucker punch. He definitely hadn't helped, with all his comments over the past few weeks about how important family was to him and how he planned to give Abby siblings one day…all the while kissing Hannah on his front porch and daydreaming of a future with her. Talk about rubbing it in her face.

Yet she knew the truth, all that time—and never said a word. If she hadn't come in here defending CREATE and the art department, would she have ever told him? Or would she have just let him pursue her endlessly, with no explanations as to her constant rejection—even knowing his own vulnerabilities from the past?

"It's pretty obvious I'm not what you want, Jude. I told you before—I'm not what you need." Hannah grabbed the bag and made her way toward the door. She hesitated, then added one last shattering truth with a pointed gaze to his computer. "And after this conversation, I'm starting to realize you're not what I need, either."

Chapter Eighteen

"I'm sick." Hannah coughed into the phone later that night, her words not completely a lie as she did have a sore throat from crying, and nausea from the incessant headache that had plagued her ever since leaving Jude's office earlier that afternoon. She'd collected herself in the bathroom, made her magazine distributions—despite knowing they were pointless—and came straight home, where she'd collapsed on the couch with a spoon and pint of ice cream and hadn't budged since.

And had zero intentions of doing so.

"You were fine earlier." Sophia's confused tone rang over the line. "What happened? Did you pick up a bug delivering magazines?"

"Something like that." More like picked up a broken heart. Hannah ran a hand over her forehead as a fresh wave of misery poured over her. She still couldn't believe she'd blurted her long-kept secret from Jude that way, but it'd been time. Past time, actually. Now he knew the truth, and could leave her alone.

That fact made her head throb in heavy rhythm with her heart. "I don't think I can make it the rest of this week teaching." Hannah hesitated. "Can you finish the photography session on your own?"

"It can't be that serious," Sophia argued. Running water sounded in the background. She was probably washing paint out of her brushes again, something she always did on the phone to multitask. "What about the CREATE meeting Friday? This is crunch time. We have to get moving on the first round of fundraisers. The bake sale is in a week, and you promised the kids you'd help, remember? Besides, no one cares if you're blowing your nose every few minutes."

The clatter of brushes knocking together only reminded Hannah of the inevitable doom coming her friend's way on Monday night—the one that would end, or at best, stall her beloved career. She couldn't believe she'd all but promised Jude would do the right thing. How could she have been so naive? So blind?

Hannah groaned. "It's more serious than nose blowing."

"How? It's not flu season yet."

"Worse than that."

The water shut off. "Hannah, spit it out. What's going on?"

She took a deep breath. "I talked to Jude."

An expectant silence pulsed over the line.

Hannah licked her lips, knowing Sophia wouldn't say anything until she told the entire story. So she did, in several run-on sentences, starting with the minute she bumped into Russell in the teachers' lounge and ending with the flavor of ice cream melting in her lap.

When Sophia finally spoke, her voice pulled more tautly than a tightrope. "Let me get this straight. You're saying you can't finish the class with me because you don't want to run into Jude? After all we've been through together the last month at that school? After all that's coming my way in a few days?"

Guilt burned Hannah's insides—but not as potently as the embarrassment and regret that still lingered. "I can't see him right now—or Abby. There's no telling what she's going to think." Abby. Great. One more stolen piece of the puzzle Hannah had started piecing together in her heart.

This was going to hurt even more than she thought.

God, where is Romans 8? I'm so lost.

"So you're going to hide the truth from Abby after harping on Jude for doing the same about her mom?" Frustration tinged Sophia's tone. "Where's that faith you were preaching about earlier? One more wave in life knocked you over, and your religion is gone again, just like that. Washed away. No wonder I've never felt comfortable in church." She snorted. "At least I'm consistent with my unbelief."

Hannah's stomach clenched. "Sophia—"

"No." Her friend cut her off. "You do whatever you think you need to do. But don't blame it on being sick or on anything other than the truth. You're afraid, and you're a hypocrite."

The words stung, but the reality of them bled Hannah's heart. Sophia had a point—a good one. What kind of witness was she being to her friend when Hannah couldn't handle anything negative? Wasn't she just pondering the depth of her renewed faith earlier that very afternoon?

She squeezed her eyes shut. *Okay, God. No more playing around. I'm here to stay.* She gulped. *Regardless.*

Starting with the hard stuff.

Hannah opened her eyes and released a shaky breath into the phone. "Okay. I'll be there Friday as planned."

God, help me.

It'd been the longest week of Jude's life. Well, no, that was the first week after Miranda left, when he wondered minute by minute if her choice would be permanent or temporary. But this separation from Hannah hurt in a different way, one just as profound.

And Abby felt it, too.

"Did you and Ms. Hart have a fight?" Abby

turned to him, sugar cookie dough smeared on her cheek where she'd snuck a taste of the batter before he warned her about the raw eggs. She'd coerced him into a Sunday night baking session, something he'd normally try to talk her out of, but with Abby's down mood of late—not to mention his own—he figured a little bonding over sprinkles couldn't hurt.

It somehow made Hannah's presence that much more stark.

"Not exactly." He grabbed the cookie sheet from the drawer below the oven, then opened a cabinet.

"Then where has she been? And why was she so upset Friday in class?" Abby selected a cookie cutter his parents had given her one Christmas from the pile and began making flower shapes in the dough.

Jude finally found the nonstick spray in the drawer by the fridge, and gave the cookie sheet a thorough dousing. "Stuff has come up, honey." The stuff movies were made of. Even if the art department's cut wasn't a slap in Hannah's face, she sure left her own handprint on Jude's cheek. Unable to have kids—did she really think something like that would keep him from pursuing her? Did he seem that surface-level? Sure, he'd have to adjust to the idea of not adding to his family, and it hurt she hadn't told him sooner, but why did it have to be all or nothing? Adoption was a ready solution, one that had grown on him ever since hearing Hannah say the words that apparently changed everything for her.

Just not for him.

Still, was he supposed to chase after her and tell her that? Jude had made it clear he'd hoped to have more kids one day, but he'd never given the impression that he valued future, invisible children over his next marriage.

"Dad." Abby dropped the cookie cutter and put her hands on her hips, her expression too knowing for her own good. "I'm not a little kid. I know when something is up." She hesitated, nibbling her bottom lip. "Is she going to come back over soon?"

Jude sighed as he returned the spray to the cabinet. He should have known better than to hide the truth again. "We had a disagreement." To put it mildly. He shut the cabinet door. "And we were just friends, Abby. Nothing more." Though he thought they were making progress, but Hannah had never intended to get serious. Was there another reason? Maybe the infertility was just an excuse not to want to get hurt again.

Though the tears in her eyes had certainly been real enough, regardless of the motive behind them.

"Then say you're sorry and get her back over here already." Abby rolled her eyes like it was that easy, reminding Jude that she might be grown up in many ways, but not in all of them.

"I wish I could. But there's more to it than that." He picked up a heart-shaped cookie cutter and twirled it around his finger. "I can't really talk about it."

"More secrets?" Abby snatched the cutter from his hand and shoved it against the dough, harder than necessary. "I thought you'd be sick of those by now."

"I am. Trust me." Jude winced as she doggedly made heart after heart. "But some secrets aren't mine to tell."

"So you're not keeping anything from me now? Nothing at all?" Her eyes met his and held in a challenge. He couldn't say no without lying, not with the proposal for tomorrow night's meeting practically burning a hole in his briefcase.

"Actually, there is something we should discuss, now that it's about to become official." He spoke softly, hoping to diffuse the anger slowly drawing Abby's features together like a rubber band. "It's about the meeting tomorrow…" His voice trailed off, making it easy for Abby to fill in the blanks.

"You're getting rid of CREATE, aren't you?" Her spine stiffened, and she started slapping cut out dough onto the cookie sheet. She didn't wait for an answer before barreling on. "No wonder Ms. Hart is mad at you."

"That's not—"

Abby dropped another heart on the sheet with surprising calm. "It doesn't matter, Dad. We worked really hard on that magazine, and we're going to prove you wrong. We'll save the art department—with or without you."

He reared back, not just at her words, but with the determination feeding them. Abby really believed in her club's efforts, and he had to admit, they'd all worked hard—not only on the magazine, but in planning constant events throughout the remainder of the school year to keep funds flowing. Cake walks, bake sales, car washes—CREATE and even members outside of the club were willing to dive in and do their part to save the art department. No one from the sports teams had shown such dedication, probably because they knew they weren't really in danger.

Then there was Russell, whose faith in God bolstered him enough to know things would work out the way they should regardless of whether he stressed over the details or not. Jude had a lot to learn from both CREATE and his friend.

Not to mention Hannah.

Her words rang in his ears even now. *You always have a choice.* Did he? Maybe so. Maybe he'd been blinded to more than what was best for the majority. Maybe he needed to narrow his scope a little. After all, God had put this responsibility on him, ready or not, and he had yet to feel a peace in his heart about his decision. Was that a sign? It was time to start doing more listening and less griping, that was for sure. Time to do a lot of things.

Hannah's words echoed in his head. *It's pretty obvious I'm not what you want. I'm not what you need.*

Time to prove Hannah wrong on both accounts.

He'd let pride and rejection be his companions far too long. Miranda might have taken a lot with her that day she sailed out the door forever, but he refused to let her take another moment of happiness from his and Abby's future. Not when he could help it.

Jude stole a glance at his briefcase, propped on the kitchen counter by the coffeepot ready for him to grab Monday on his way to work, and an idea struck—one that just might solve both of his problems. Maybe Abby was right. Maybe they could save the arts with or without him.

But he chose with.

Chapter Nineteen

Standing room only. Jude resisted the urge to wipe his slightly sweaty palms down the legs of his slacks as he cast a cursory glance at the crowd below him in the auditorium of the school. He refused to gauge their expressions, refused to read the papers in his hand for the hundredth time— refused to do anything other than focus on the fact that in a mere thirty minutes or less, this entire semester's worth of stress would be over.

The outcome, however, could create an entirely new list of reasons for high blood pressure. But again, he couldn't go there now. He had to do what he had to do, regardless of the results.

Though he really wished Hannah had at least come to hear them.

As Principal Coleman droned on with his seemingly endless opening remarks, Jude's gaze flickered over Abby, still pouting on the third row with a group of her friends and their parents. He strained to see the back of the room. But his favorite head of silky brown hair was nowhere to be seen—and neither were Sophia's fiery red curls. He'd thought surely she'd be here—it certainly seemed the rest of the town had shown up. His eyes darted over the first row of attendees—the board members—and he quickly averted his gaze away from their stern expressions, tuning back to the presentation just in time.

"I'll now turn the stage over to Vice Principal Bradley, who will present the proposed solution for the budget crisis." Principal Coleman stepped back from the podium and gestured for Jude to take his spot.

Here went nothing. Or maybe everything. Jude nodded at Coleman with a confidence he didn't feel and strode to the podium, where he laid his carefully prepared speech. After making his decision last night, he'd pored over the right words to use, knowing that with his new plan, it'd take more than hard data and research to convince the board to go with it. It'd take heart and passion, and with Hannah avoiding him the past week, he was severely lacking both.

Jude cleared his throat, then leaned toward the microphone, his introduction thankfully memorized. "Thank you all for showing up tonight. Your interest and support of the electives at Pecan Grove help make this school what it is today."

The sea of grim faces before him didn't smile,

and a momentary wave of panic washed over Jude. What if his last-minute switch had been a bad idea? What if he was about to create a mob scene? He swallowed, debating whether to move forward or default to his old plan. If Hannah had given up on him already, if Abby had written him off, what was there to lose now? He hadn't told Abby about the proposal change for this very reason—in case he couldn't do it.

Jude briefly closed his eyes, his heartbeat thundering in his ears, highlighted by the expectant silence of the auditorium. *God, some wisdom would be great right about now.* He'd prayed over his decision into the wee hours last night, but obviously, it hadn't been enough to kick the doubts.

The back doors opened, squeaking on their hinges, and a shaft of light lit the shadows of the back row—and a figure silhouetted in the frame. Jude sucked in his breath. Hannah.

A fresh dose of inspiration flooded Jude's veins, and he relaxed for the first time in weeks as Hannah and Sophia slipped inside and stood against the back wall. She'd come. She was frowning, and her arms were crossed, but she was here.

That was all the sign he needed.

Jude ditched his speech, deciding to speak with the sincerity he'd felt when writing it instead of with the actual words. "Most of you think you already know what I'm going to say—but you're probably wrong."

He wished he could see Hannah's expression from this far away, but maybe that was for the best. Jude licked his dry lips and pressed forward, coming around from behind the podium to address the crowd one-on-one. "The elective departments are important to all of us—staff, parents and the community alike. But I think we might be forgetting that they're even more important to the students."

A mumble of agreement went through the crowd, bolstering Jude's confidence. He directed his attention to the board members, most of whom were leaning forward with interest. "I've spent the last several weeks trying to find the data to prove the sports department deserved to be saved. But you know what?" He spread his hands wide. "I couldn't find it."

Another ripple sounded through the auditorium, this one with angry undertones. Hannah's slumped position against the wall straightened, and the hope he felt in that single movement gave Jude the courage to continue. "Several students from the art department and the after-school club, CREATE, began a series of fundraisers, including designing, printing and selling their own magazine for the cause—using the skills they learned from the club."

"Yeah—and one of 'em is your own daughter," a disgruntled voice yelled from somewhere in the middle of the rows of seats.

Jude held up both hands against the murmurs of indignation, ignoring Coleman stiffening on stage to his right. He could handle this—for the first time this year, he knew he truly could handle it. "That's true. Abby is in the club. But her involvement didn't give me bias. If anything, my personal past did—*against* the art department." He let out a slow breath. "Abby, and the rest of CREATE, showed me how hard they were willing to work to save their club. How much time, energy and effort they were willing to sacrifice for something that might prove pointless." Abby caught his eyes from the third row, and a bashful smile broke across her face. "They had a nearly impossible goal before them, yet strove forward without fear of failure."

He smiled back before his eyes flickered to Hannah. "Not only did the students go above and beyond, but they were directed by selfless, intelligent teachers and volunteers who were willing and able to guide them toward their goals and help them use their talents for a cause they believed in."

The auditorium fell silent again, but frowns still existed on more faces than not. Jude eased back behind the podium, bracing his arms on each side. "The electives have been in danger during this unfortunate period. But the art club stepped forward and decided to do something about it, and I believe that deserves to be recognized."

A handful of people began to clap halfheartedly, while others remained stoic with arms crossed.

Jude brushed off the applause, and it fell short. "That said, I've changed my proposal to something that I feel is not only fair, but in the best interest of every student in this school, regardless of their personal interests."

To his right, Coleman coughed, probably afraid of how this was going to go, but Jude ignored him and kept on. "My proposal tonight is to keep both departments—sports and art."

"That's impossible." The board president shook his head as several other protests sounded throughout the room.

Coleman had had enough. He stalked to Jude's side, covered the microphone with one hand, and hissed in his ear. "What are you doing?"

"Trust me." Jude didn't bother to whisper back, and Coleman reluctantly released the microphone and eased into the background. "I propose that both departments are given equal funding from the remainder of the budget allowance, and the deficits for each group be made up by student-hosted fundraisers given throughout the year."

The drone of the room increased to an uproar, though the majority of the voices this time seemed positive and encouraging. Jude raised his voice to be heard over the din. "All of the students could stand to learn from the example provided to them by the members of CREATE, and their leaders, art teacher Sophia Davis and especially volunteer Hannah

Hart." He inhaled deeply and hoped Hannah could read his heart from this far away. "I know I have."

Hannah stared in disbelief as the crowd in the auditorium, ready to sentence Jude mere moments ago, stood to their feet and applauded for him— including the school board on the front row. But all she could hear was her name dripping off Jude's lips. He'd publicly thanked her—even after the way she'd gone off on him, attacked him with not only her personal opinion regarding school business, but with the baggage from her past. She'd all but slammed Jude upside the head with a fully packed suitcase, and he'd still heard her—and respected her enough to take her thoughts into consideration.

"You were right." Sophia's voice in her ear jerked Hannah back to reality as Jude humbly thanked the audience and made his way off stage. "I'm sorry I didn't give him more credit."

"I didn't, either." Hannah watched as Jude shook hands with the board members, her stomach pinching as a variety of emotions coursed through her body, racking her nerves. "I was wrong, too."

"He obviously changed his mind from last week." Sophia nudged Hannah with her hip, her oversize bag brushing Hannah's side. "I'm pretty sure you had something to do with it."

"I don't see how. I just yelled." Hannah shrugged, biting her lip as the memories of her words flooded her with guilt. "Then threw my fears in his face and left." Left *him*. No wonder he hadn't come after her—he'd already had one woman he cared about walk away. What did she expect? Hannah had ripped open that old wound in her dramatic exit as well. Regardless of the school board's final decision, tonight had proved one thing—Jude had class.

And Hannah did not.

"He really likes you, Hannah. Don't throw it away because of the past." Sophia tucked the lock of hair covering Hannah's scarred cheek behind her ear and smiled. "Yours or his."

Before Hannah could argue, Sophia sucked in her breath. "Time for my exit. Fill me in later." She disappeared into the throngs of people beginning to exit the auditorium.

Hannah called after her. "Sophia! Wait. Where—"

"You made it." Jude's warm voice answered the questions left in Sophia's peach scented wake, and Hannah slowly turned to face him for the first time since telling him off in his office—again.

"That was quite the presentation." She offered a hesitant smile, reaching up on habit to smooth her hair over her cheek, then let her hand drop to her side instead. She had nothing to hide anymore. With Jude, she never did.

But it was too late.

"I'm glad you heard it." Jude's cologne wafted toward her as he pressed closer in order to be heard over the din of people leaving the auditorium. "I was afraid you weren't coming."

"I almost didn't. Sophia made me." Hannah realized belatedly how childish her words sounded, but they were the truth. "Did you really mean what you said up there?" She gestured to the stage where the board members were talking with ducked heads to Principal Coleman.

"Every word." Jude let out a breath of embarrassment as he held up several sheets of paper. "This was the speech I was *supposed* to read. But I got the point out, I suppose."

"You did really well." Hannah's heart pulsed an extra beat at Jude's proximity, followed by a wave of pain so strong it almost buckled her knees. She'd never get to be this close again, never get to brush his fingers through the hair above his shirt collar again.

"Hannah…" Jude's voice trailed off and his fingers lightly brushed her scar. Against her better judgment, she leaned into the strength of his hand. "What you told me in my office last week—I don't care."

She stiffened under his hand, and it fell to his side.

"That didn't come out right." Jude rocked back on his heels, seemingly as lost without touching her as she felt without his touch. He shoved his hands into his pockets. "I meant, I don't mind. Maybe I did a little at first—it was certainly a shock. But that has nothing to do with how I feel about you."

Hannah shook her head, her hair swishing across her shoulders and tickling her cheek that still felt cold in his absence. "You say that now." Her fiancé had changed his mind, even after reaching a level of commitment Jude hadn't yet aspired to.

A shadow crept over Jude's expression. "I'm very serious. I won't change my mind."

"You will. Believe me." An invisible vise seemed to squeeze Hannah from both sides, nearly robbing her of the words she wished she didn't have to say. "They always do."

Jude frowned, his eyebrows meshing together into a tight line. "Who is *they?*"

"My ex-fiancé." Hannah flapped her hand in a vain attempt to quit blurting out her most painful secrets at the worst possible time. Here she was, in the middle of what should be a celebration for the school, and all she wanted to do was cry. Again. "After he found out…" Tears choked her throat, and she couldn't say more.

A tiny light of understanding lit Jude's eyes. But he didn't really understand. No one could. "Hannah, I had no—"

"Dad!" Abby squealed as she rushed up the aisle behind Jude and wrapped her arms around his waist in a bear hug. "I can't believe it! Thank you, thank you, thank you!"

Hannah took advantage of the distraction to dab her eyes with her sleeve, and had a ready smile in place by the time Abby turned her beaming grin toward her. "Congratulations, Abby. You guys earned this." She nodded toward Jude, careful not to look at him. "And if I understood right, you'll have to keep earning it."

"No problem!" Abby slapped Hannah a high five. "We got this now."

"I fully believe you do." Her smile felt a little more genuine this time.

Jude turned on what Hannah now recognized as his father voice. "Abby, the board said nothing is official until they vote at their next meeting."

Abby's smile fell slightly.

Jude let loose with a slow grin. "But they also said I should have no reason to expect anything other than a unanimous vote for the proposal."

"You're the best, Dad." Abby hugged Jude again, and Hannah knew if she didn't leave now, she'd break down—and there wouldn't be enough sleeves in the entire room to dry the river threatening to pour.

"I'll see you guys later. I need to find Sophia—she's my ride." Hannah blew a kiss at Abby, and allowed one final glance at Jude. "Goodbye."

Pain stoked his eyes, but Hannah only ducked her head and filed out the door with the remaining drifters from the meeting. She'd find Sophia, go home and concentrate on the good Jude had done tonight.

And somehow, try to figure out how her heart would keep beating.

"We need a plan." Abby licked her celebratory ice cream, her tongue covered in rainbow sprinkles.

"I agree." Jude stared at his melting chocolate cone, his appetite gone despite the positive outcome of the meeting. The good news had been soured by the realization that Hannah truly believed he didn't care enough to weather a storm at her side.

But it sounded as if she had good reason to believe so. No wonder she refused to let Jude too close. He'd been burned by Miranda, but Hannah been singed just as bad in her own way. How could her ex have ditched her after finding out something so tragic? What kind of commitment had he made, anyway? Good thing they'd never made it to the altar, because obviously that loser had no idea of the meaning of "for better or for worse."

Jude and Hannah had definitely both been hurt in the past, but there was nothing stopping them from moving on—together. It just seemed now Hannah was bent on moving forward alone. It'd taken Jude nearly ten years to move on with his life—he didn't wish the same on Hannah. In fact, he'd do whatever it took to convince her she was worth pursuing, regardless of her scars—external or internal.

He focused on Abby. "Got any bright ideas?" During the drive to get ice cream, he'd finally answered his daughter's questions about Hannah. Not the personal details about her accident, but the gist of why Hannah had stopped coming over. Abby had demanded they work it out, claiming Hannah was the best match for both of them.

"What about renting one of those planes with the banners?" Abby waved her cone, sending a layer of sprinkles across the table. "Or a message on the big screen at a ball game, like they do on TV!" Her voice rose with excitement.

Jude hated to put a damper on her creativity, but one of those options was beyond his meager salary, the other impossible as Pecan Grove didn't have a professional sports arena. "Think small scale, big impact."

Abby twitched her lips to the side. Jude went back to staring at his cone. He couldn't bear to lose Hannah permanently—he knew they would be good together. He'd helped her begin to overcome the insecurities of her scarred cheek, and she'd shown him how to move forward. To accept that beauty lay in the eye of the beholder, not necessarily in the cover of a magazine. That his daughter's beauty was nothing to fear. That he *was* a good parent, just in need of loosening up.

Ice cream dripped on his finger, yet he still

stared. If it hadn't been for Hannah, he'd still be at odds with Abby, still be flinching with every click of a camera shutter and avoiding the dusty scrapbooks in the attic. Would still be living in the black and white of the past and fearing the future. No, he couldn't lose Hannah now.

Not when she'd finally shown him how to live in color.

"I got it!" Abby jumped forward again, jerking Jude's arm braced against the table. His cone splattered to the tabletop.

"What?" He grabbed a handful of napkins as Abby continued bouncing in her seat.

"It's perfect!" She leaned forward and blurted out the details of her plan. Jude sat back in his seat, clutching a handful of messy napkins and not minding in the least.

It *was* perfect.

Sophia so owed her.

Hannah hurried toward the playground equipment at the park, trying not to think about the last time she'd been here when Abby had tagged along with her friend. Thoughts of the girl—and her dad—only made Hannah's stomach churn again, and she'd already spent the entire week living on antacids.

The sun set behind the bank of trees to the west, and Hannah picked up her pace. Hopefully the light would hold out long enough to get set up. The sunset would be the perfect backdrop for a Friday evening shoot, and with the park mostly deserted as families headed home for dinner, she should be able to take her new client's photos quickly.

Though not as quickly as if Sophia had agreed to help her. Hannah frowned as she walked around an abandoned soccer ball left in the empty field by the swings. After the weeks Hannah had spent teaching, one would think her friend would be a little more amiable to her request for help. Oh, well, maybe it was time to consider hiring a real assistant, so she and Sophia could quit playing favor-tag. She definitely wouldn't be going back to Pecan Grove Junior High anytime soon.

Hannah stopped by a two-story slide and brushed her hair back from her face, wishing she'd worn a warmer sweater as she scanned the area for her new client. A young family, they'd said in the email she received from her website, who needed portraits to celebrate a new addition. Maybe someone had recently had a baby. But who would bring a tiny baby out to a park at sunset, in the chill of an autumn evening?

Apprehension tickled Hannah's spine, and she gripped the strap of her camera bag tighter. Maybe she should have investigated her new client a little more before just showing up. She'd never had issues in the past, but something didn't add up here.

Movement on the far side of the park caught her attention—an adult and a teenager, their backs to her as they pumped their legs and swung. Hannah relaxed, shaking her head at her unfounded fears, and moved toward the duo. This must be them—but where was the baby? And the other parent?

"Hello there!" she called as she got closer, casting a worried eye at her rapidly fading light. "Are you waiting for Hannah Hart?"

The figures stopped pumping, letting their feet drag the hard-packed dirt to stop the swings. She drew closer as the adult figure easily slipped off one swing and landed on his feet.

His loafer-clad feet.

Jude smiled at her as Abby joined his side, beaming. "We sure are—have been for most of our lives, I'd say."

Instant tears burned the back of Hannah's throat, and she pressed her lips together. She couldn't cry. Couldn't allow herself to feel. But oh, how she wanted to fall into Jude's arms and let his whispered assurances be all she needed.

But if she really loved him, she'd let him go. Let him be free to start a family, to find a woman who could give him his dreams and make him forget his past once and for all. He needed someone without baggage.

And she had a whole airport terminal full.

Jude strolled toward her, Abby at his heels. Then before Hannah could protest, Abby slipped the camera bag off Hannah's arm. "I'll take this." She positioned it carefully in both hands and hurried away.

"What's going on?" Hannah started to look back to see where Abby was carting away her means of making a living, but Jude gently turned her face back to his with a soft touch on her chin. She stared at him, a dozen questions roiling in her mind. She finally blurted one out. "Are you the new client that emailed me?"

"Pretty clever, huh?" Humor lit Jude's eyes, startling blue against the navy long-sleeved dress shirt he must have worn to work. "That was all Abby's idea. We thought we should return to the scene of the crime—where that picture you took of her started it all."

So she hadn't been the only one remembering that day. Hannah averted her gaze from Jude's, wishing she was strong enough to fight the memories, to walk out of his arms and back to her car. Back home, where it was safe.

And lonely.

She steeled her spine against the brisk wind that rustled the tree branches—and against the man before her. "So what was all that about a new addition? Just part of the lie?"

"It's you, Hannah." Jude brought his hands up to cup her face, and despite knowing better, she inhaled deeply of his cologne, of his unique scent that left her craving more. "We want you."

"I told you, I'm not what you need." Hannah closed her eyes, unable to look into his earnest expression any longer. "I can't have kids, and you want a big family. I'm scarred, Jude, in more ways than one."

"So am I." He wiped a rogue tear off her cheek and waited until she opened her eyes. "But we'll get through all that together. I'm not promising anything will be perfect. I'm not promising I won't still get overprotective with Abby sometimes, and I can't promise I won't ever lose my temper. But I'm trying. With God's help, I'll do better every day."

His heartfelt eagerness only made the tears flow faster. Such a good man—and still so off-limits. If she really loved Jude, she couldn't let him settle. Not after all he'd been through. He deserved the best—and with their differences, that wasn't her. "Your faults aren't the ones in question here."

"Listen, I know your fiancé hurt you. And that makes me wish I could hurt him." Jude shook his head, his hands trailing from her cheeks to her shoulders and squeezing lightly. She felt the warmth all the way to her toes. "But that factor aside, I'm more than open to adoption in the future. I don't care—I want *you,* Hannah. Not what you can or can't give me." He lifted her chin with one finger, arresting her gaze with his own. "So I'm asking you again. Will you give me a chance to prove that to you?"

"What if you regret it?" Hannah's resolve weakened as his gaze darted to her lips, then back to her eyes. She shivered, and not just from the cold. "What if in five years you resent me?"

"How do I know you won't walk out the door one day and not come back?" Jude shrugged. "We can't tell the future, Hannah. That's where our trust in God has to come into play. But I do know one thing…" His voice trailed off as he fished in his shirt pocket and pulled out a small box. Then he knelt before her on the leaf-scattered ground. "Abby and I want you in every picture we take for the rest of our lives."

The entire park seemed to hold its breath. The wind stilled, leaving the branches silent and the fallen leaves mute. The sunset behind her sent beams of light streaking through the treetops, and cast a spotlight on the diamond shining up at her, beckoning her to believe. To stop hiding. To trust.

Then a sudden gust of wind filled her spirit, whispering truth. *Let me work things for good…*

Jude waited patiently, eyes locked on Hannah's, never wavering despite what had to be an uncomfortable position on the ground. His gaze radiated sincerity. Confidence.

Love.

Hannah inhaled deeply, her heart lodged in her throat, afraid to say yes—yet somehow even more afraid to say no. She was tired of living in a still-life portrait. She wanted vivid. Movement. Bright colors. How could she truly live the rest of her life without Jude and Abby in each snapshot? It was risky—there'd surely be more bad times, more storms.

But she couldn't image weathering them with a better team.

Faith. I want to have faith, God.

A slow smile broke across Hannah's face, until she felt it clear through her heart. "Yes."

Jude's eyes lit with delight and he quickly stood and pulled her against him. He slipped the ring onto her finger then landed a solid kiss on her lips—just as a flash of white light nearly blinded Hannah.

"Got it!" Sophia's familiar laugh rang from somewhere beside them. Hannah turned away from Jude and the diamond glittering on her finger, to see her best friend and Abby on the top platform of the jungle gym, holding Hannah's camera and grinning like she'd won a photography award.

"You guys…" Hannah shook her head and laughed as Abby slid down the closest slide and ran toward her. She'd totally been had. And had loved every minute of it.

Abby's skinny arms locked around Hannah's waist, and Hannah leaned over to breathe in the sunshine-laden scent of her hair. Then she pulled back to look into Abby's face. "I said yes to you, too, you know."

Abby smiled, pure adoration shining in her eyes. "I know." Then her smile faded slightly. "Will you be my mom now?"

Hannah's breath caught. "Would you like that?"

"More than anything else in the world." Abby's voice dropped to a whisper and Hannah clutched her tighter. "And not just because you're a super awesome photographer."

Hannah held back a laugh, hugging Abby tight as Jude wrapped his arms around both of them. Another flash lit the playground as Sophia recorded the moment for eternity. Talk about a family portrait. This would go perfectly in the living room in Jude's house—or maybe above the fireplace in a new home they'd buy together. She didn't care where they lived, as long as these two people were her family.

Jude raised his head from the group hug and smiled at Hannah over Abby's hair. "I love you." His eyes spoke the truth even deeper than his words, and she hoped he could read the return message in her own gaze.

"I love you, too."

The sun finished setting behind the trees, its golden beams highlighting Jude and Abby—and their newest addition—in one final burst of light before slowly giving way to shadows. As Hannah reveled in the embrace of her new family, she thanked God for not only providing her with the deepest desires of her heart—but with providing her with His never-ending light. She might not be able to control her future, but with God working even the bad times for good, she had no reason to ever fear the shadows again.

* * * * *

Dear Reader,

When I first began this story, I wanted to write a tale of a female photographer and name her after my friend, who took fantastic photos of my daughter on her second birthday. I became intrigued with the whole photography concept. But the story took an unexpected twist when the heroine in the story showed up with a scar. It resonated with me, because while many of us might not have physical scars on the surface, we all have interior scars we try to cover—such as regrets, unfulfilled dreams, even infertility. These scars tempt us to live life in shades of black and gray; in shadows instead of in light. But what if we embraced those scars and came to realize that God still has a plan for us? What if we let them serve as positive reminders instead of negative blemishes? I challenge you, Dear Reader, to stop hiding and start seeking the One who made us exactly as we are. Like Hannah finally did in the story, come out from behind the camera—and live your life in full color.

Betsy St. Amant

Questions for Discussion

1. In the story, Jude fears that his daughter will pick up the negative traits left by his ex-wife. Do you feel his fears were founded or unfounded?

2. Do you think it's possible for fears, whether rational or irrational, to control our lives? How can we stop this from happening?

3. Hannah struggled with her physical appearance and self-confidence because of the scar she received from a car wreck. Have you ever let something you couldn't control about your physical appearance consume your life or daily thoughts?

4. As an almost-teenager, Abby had a lot of learning to do about true beauty. What do you think defines true beauty?

5. Hannah took Abby under her wing and showed her that having a good heart on the inside made your outside appearance that much prettier. How could Hannah have taken her own advice? Why is it sometimes easy to "talk the talk" instead of "walking the walk"?

6. It's not easy being a single father—but how did Jude's overprotective drive backfire on him regarding his daughter?

7. Jude and Hannah were instantly attracted to each other, but had significant obstacles in their path to work through individually before ever having a chance to make it as a couple. Have you ever met someone—whether a romantic relationship or friendship—that inspired you to make a change in your life for the better?

8. In the story, the art department was pitted against the sports department for use of the depleting school funds. If you had been in Jude's position, which department would you have chosen to save? Or would you have made the same choice he did? Why?

9. Hannah's faith took a nosedive after her car accident. Do you allow the storms of life to mold you for good, or do you tend to carry the bitterness around for years, like Hannah? Why?

10. Hannah's best friend, Sophia, was instrumental in being there for Hannah in the aftermath of her wreck. Have you ever had a friend who stood by you through bad times in life? How did they help support you, and how can you return the favor one day?

11. Though at first shy, Hannah ended up thriving while helping teach Sophia's art class and working with the students in the after-school club. How can turning our focus away from ourselves and toward others help us weather life's storms? What can you do to make that step today?

12. Hannah always wanted a big family, but was robbed of being able to have one because of her accident. She later decided adoption would be the way to go. Do you know anyone who has adopted? Would you ever consider adopting children if placed in Hannah's position or otherwise?

13. Leaving behind a legacy and a family name was important to Jude, because of his own childhood. However, Hannah wrongly mistook that desire as something Jude viewed as more important than her. Have you ever had to sacrifice a dream because of a relationship? How did you handle it?

14. Hannah had a hard time believing Jude really wanted to be with her forever, because she knew she could never have kids. She let her own insecurities cloud her reality. Have you ever had this happen to you? How can we stay in control of

our emotions, rather than let our emotions and past experiences blind us to the truth?

15. Hannah's passion in life is photography. What hobby or career path would you choose, if you were guaranteed to have success?

SUSPENSE

RIVETING INSPIRATIONAL ROMANCE

Watch for our series of edge-
of-your-seat suspense novels.
These contemporary tales
of intrigue and romance
feature Christian characters
facing challenges to their faith...
and their lives!

**AVAILABLE IN REGULAR
& LARGER-PRINT FORMATS**

For exciting stories that reflect traditional values,
visit:
www.ReaderService.com